I0679630

ALL IN IT
"K (1)" Carries On

TO
ALL SECOND LIEUTENANTS
AND IN PARTICULAR TO
THE MEMORY OF
ONE SECOND LIEUTENANT

ALL IN IT
"K (1)"
Carries On

BY

IAN HAY

Boston and New York
Houghton Mifflin Company
The Riverside Press Cambridge

COPYRIGHT, 1917, BY IAN HAY BEITH

ALL RIGHTS RESERVED

Published November 1917

AUTHOR'S NOTE

The First Hundred Thousand closed with the Battle of Loos. The present narrative follows certain friends of ours from the scene of that costly but valuable experience, through a winter campaign in the neighbourhood of Ypres and Ploegsteert, to profitable participation in the Battle of the Somme.

Much has happened since then. The initiative has passed once and for all into our hands; so has the command of the air. Russia has been reborn, and, like most healthy infants, is passing through an uproarious period of teething trouble; but now America has stepped in, and promises to do more than redress the balance. All along the Western Front we have begun to move forward, without haste or flurry, but in such wise that during the past twelve months no position, once fairly captured and consolidated, has ever been regained by the enemy. To-day you can stand upon certain recently won eminences — Wytchaete Ridge, Messines Ridge, Vimy Ridge, and Monchy — looking down into the enemy's lines, and looking forward to the territory which yet remains to be restored to France.

You can also look back — not merely from these ridges, but from certain moral ridges as well — over the ground which has been successfully traversed, and you can marvel for the hundredth time, not that the thing was well or badly done, but that it was ever done at all.

But while this narrative was being written, none of these things had happened. We were still struggling uphill, with inadequate resources. So, since the incidents of the story were set down, in the main, as they occurred and when they occurred, the reader will find very little perspective, a great deal of the mood of the moment, and none at all of that profound wisdom which comes after the event. For the latter he must look home — to the lower walks of journalism and the back benches of the House of Commons.

It is not proposed to carry this story to a third volume. The First Hundred Thousand, as such, are no more. Like the "Old Contemptibles," they are now merged in a greater and more victorious army — in an armed nation, in fact. And, as Sergeant Mucklewame once observed to me, "There's no that mony of us left now, onyways." So with all reverence — remembering how, when they were needed most, these men did not pause to reason why or count the cost, but came at once — we bid them good-bye.

CONTENTS

All In It

"K (1)" Carries On

I

WINTER QUARTERS

I

WE are getting into our stride again. Two months ago we trudged into Bethune, gaunt, dirty, soaked to the skin, and reduced to a comparative handful. None of us had had his clothes off for a week. Our ankle-puttees had long dropped to pieces, and our hose-tops, having worked under the soles of our boots, had been cut away and discarded. The result was a bare and mud-splashed expanse of leg from boot to kilt, except in the case of the enterprising few who had devised artistic spat-puttees out of an old sandbag. Our headgear consisted in a few cases of the regulation Balmoral bonnet, usually minus "toorie" and badge; in a few more, of the battered remains of a gas helmet; and in the great majority, of a woollen cap-comforter. We were bearded like that incomparable fighter, the *poilu*, and we were separated by an abyss of years, so our stomachs told us, from our last square meal.

But we were wonderfully placid about it all. Our regimental pipers, who had come out to play us in, were making what the Psalmist calls "a joyful noise" in front; and behind us lay the recollection of a battle, still raging, in which we had struck the first blow, and borne our full share for three days and nights. Moreover, our particular blow had bitten deeper into the enemy's line than any other blow in the neighbourhood. And, most blessed thought of all, everything was over, and we were going back to rest. For the moment, the memory of the sights we had seen, and the tax we had levied upon our bodies and souls, together with the picture of the countless sturdy lads whom we had left lying beneath the sinister shade of Fosse Eight, were beneficently obscured by the prospect of food, sleep, and comparative cleanliness.

After restoring ourselves to our personal comforts, we should doubtless go somewhere to refit. Drafts were already waiting at the Base to fill up the great gaps in our ranks. Our companies having been brought up to strength, a spate of promotions would follow. We had no Colonel, and only our Company Commander. Subalterns — what was left of them — would come by their own. N.C.O.'s, again, would have to be created by the dozen. While all this was going on, and the old names were being weeded out of the muster-roll to make way for the new, the Quartermaster would be drawing fresh equipment — packs, mess-tins, water-bottles, and the hundred oddments which always go astray in times of stress. There would be a good deal of dialogue of this sort: —

"Private M'Sumph, I see you are down for a new pack. Where is your old one?"

"Blawn off ma back, sirr!"

"Where are your puttees?"

"Blawn off ma feet, sirr!"

"Where is your iron ration?"

"Blawn oot o' ma pooch, sirr!"

"Where is your head?"

"Blawn — I beg your pardon, sirr!" — followed by generous reissues all round.

After a month or so our beloved regiment, once more at full strength, with traditions and morale annealed by the fires of experience, would take its rightful place in the forefront of "K (1)."

Such was the immediate future, as it presented itself to the wearied but optimistic brain of Lieutenant Bobby Little. He communicated his theories to Captain Wagstaffe.

"I wonder!" replied that experienced officer.

II

The chief penalty of doing a job of work well is that you are promptly put on to another. This is supposed to be a compliment.

The authorities allowed us exactly two days' rest, and then packed us off by train, with the new draft, to a particularly hot sector of the trench-line in Belgium — there to carry on with the operation known in nautical circles as "executing repairs while under steam."

Well, we have been in Belgium for two months now, and, as already stated, are getting into our stride again.

There are new faces everywhere, and some of the
old faces are not quite the same. They are finer-
drawn; one is conscious of less chubbiness all
round. War is a great maturing agent. There is,
moreover, an air of seasoned authority abroad.
Many who were second lieutenants or lance corporals three months ago are now commanding
companies and platoons. Bobby Little is in command of "A" Company: if he can cling to this
precarious eminence for thirty days — that is, if
no one is sent out to supersede him — he becomes
an "automatic" captain, aged twenty! Major
Kemp commands the battalion; Wagstaffe is his
senior major. Ayling has departed from our
midst, and rumour says that he is leading a sort of
Pooh Bah existence at Brigade Headquarters.

There are sad gaps among our old friends of the
rank and file. Ogg and Hogg, M'Slattery and
M'Ostrich, have gone to the happy hunting-
grounds. Private Dunshie, the General Specialist
(who, you may remember, found his true voca-
tion, after many days, as battalion chiropodist), is
reported "missing." But his comrades are posi-
tive that no harm has befallen him. Long experience has convinced them that in the art of landing
on his feet their departed friend has no equal.

"I doot he'll be a prisoner," suggests the faithful Mucklewame to the Transport Sergeant.

"Aye," assents the Transport Sergeant bitterly; "he'll be a prisoner. No doot he'll try to
pass himself off as an officer, for to get better
quarters!"

(The Transport Sergeant, in whose memory

certain enormities of Dunshie had rankled ever
since that versatile individual had abandoned the
veterinary profession, owing to the most excusable intervention of a pack-mule's off hind leg,
was not far out in his surmise, as subsequent history may some day reveal. But the telling of that
story is still a long way off.)

Company Sergeant-Major Pumpherston is now
Sergeant-Major of the Battalion. Mucklewame is
a corporal in his old company. Private Tosh was
"offered a stripe," too, but declined, because the
invitation did not include Private Cosh, who,
owing to a regrettable lapse not unconnected with
the rum ration, had been omitted from the Hon-
ours' List. Consequently these two grim veterans
remain undecorated, but they are objects of great
veneration among the recently joined for all that.

So you see us once more in harness, falling into
the collar with energy, if not fervour. We no
longer regard War with the least enthusiasm: we
have seen It, face to face. Our sole purpose now is
to screw our sturdy followers up to the requisite
pitch of efficiency, and keep them remorselessly
at that standard until the dawn of triumphant
and abiding peace.

We have one thing upon our side — youth.

"Most of our regular senior officers are gone,
sir," remarked Colonel Kemp one day to the
Brigadier — "dead, or wounded, or promoted to
other commands; and I have something like
twenty new subalterns. When you subtract a cen-
tenarian like myself, the average age of our Battalion Mess, including Company Commanders,

works out at something under twenty-three. But
I am not exchanging any of them, thanks!"

III

Trench-life in Belgium is an entirely different
proposition from trench-life in France. The undu‐
lating country in which we now find ourselves
offers an infinite choice of unpleasant surroundings.

Down south, Vermelles way, the trenches
stretch in a comparatively straight line for miles,
facing one another squarely, and giving little opportunity for tactical enterprise. The infantry
blaze and sputter at one another in front; the guns
roar behind; and that is all there is to be said
about it. But here, the line follows the curve of
each little hill. At one place you are in a salient,
in a trench which runs round the face of a bulging
"knowe" — a tempting target for shells of every
kind. A few hundred yards farther north, or
south, the ground is much lower, and the trench-
line runs back into a re-entrant, seeking for a position which shall not be commanded from higher
ground in front.

The line is pierced at intervals by railway-
cuttings, which have to be barricaded, and canals,
which require special defences. Almost every spot
in either line is overlooked by some adjacent ridge,
or enfiladed from some adjacent trench. It is disconcerting for a methodical young officer, after
cautiously scrutinising the trench upon his front
through a periscope, to find that the entire performance has been visible (and his entire person

exposed) to the view of a Boche trench situated
on a hill-slope upon his immediate left.

And our trench-line, with its infinity of salients
and re-entrants, is itself only part of the great
salient of "Wipers." You may imagine with what
methodical solemnity the Boche "crumps" the
interior of that constricted area. Looking round
at night, when the star-shells float up over the
skyline, one could almost imagine one's self inside
a complete circle, instead of a horseshoe.

The machine-gunners of both sides are extremely busy. In the plains of France the pursuit
of their nefarious trade was practically limited to
front-line work. When they did venture to indulge
in what they called "overhead" fire, their friends
in the forefront used to summon them after the
performance, and reproachfully point out sundry
ominous rents and abrasions in the back of the
front-line parapet. But here they can withdraw
behind a convenient ridge, and *strafe* Boches a
mile and a half away, without causing any com-
plaints. Needless to say, Brother Boche is not
backward in returning the compliment. He has
one gun in particular which never tires in its efforts to rouse us from *ennui*. It must be a long
way off, for we can only just hear the report.
Moreover, its contribution to our liveliness, when
it does arrive, falls at an extremely steep angle —
so steep, indeed, that it only just clears the embankment under which we live, and falls upon the
very doorsteps of the dug-outs with which that
sanctuary is honeycombed.

This invigorating shower is turned on regularly

for ten minutes, at three, six, nine, and twelve
o'clock daily. Its area of activity includes our
tiny but, alas! steadily growing cemetery. One
evening a regiment which had recently "taken
over" selected 6 P.M. as a suitable hour for a fu-
neral. The result was a grimly humorous spectacle — the mourners, including the Commanding
Officer and officiating clergy, taking hasty cover
in a truly novel trench; while the central figure
of the obsequies, sublimely indifferent to the Hun
and all his frightfulness, lay on the grass outside,
calm and impassive amid the whispering hail of
bullets.

As for the trenches themselves — well, as the
immortal costermonger observed, "there ain't no
word in the blooming language" for them.

In the first place, there is no settled trench-line
at all. The Salient has been a battlefield for
twelve months past. No one has ever had the
time, or opportunity, to construct anything in the
shape of permanent defences. A shallow trench,
trimmed with an untidy parapet of sandbags, and
there is your stronghold! For rest and meditation,
a hole in the ground, half-full of water and roofed
with a sheet of galvanised iron; or possibly a glori-
fied rabbit-burrow in a canal-bank. These things,
as a modern poet has observed, are all right in the
summer-time. But winter here is a disintegrating
season. It rains heavily for, say, three days. Two
days of sharp frost succeed, and the rain-soaked
earth is reduced to the necessary degree of friabil-
ity. Another day's rain, and trenches and dug-
outs come sliding down like melted butter. Even

if you revet the trenches, it is not easy to drain
them. The only difference is that if your line is
situated on the forward slope of a hill the support
trench drains into the firing-trench; if they are on
the reverse slope, the firing-trench drains into the
support trench. Our indefatigable friends Box
and Cox, of the Royal Engineers, assisted by
sturdy Pioneer Battalions, labour like heroes; but
the utmost they can achieve, in a low-lying country like this, is to divert as much water as possible
into some other Brigade's area. Which they do,
right cunningly.

In addition to the Boche, we wage continuous
warfare with the elements, and the various de-
partments of Olympus render us characteristic
assistance. The Round Game Department has
issued a set of rules for the correct method of
massaging and greasing the feet. (Major Wagstaffe refers to this as, "Sole-slapping; or What to
do in the Children's Hour; complete in Twelve
Fortnightly Parts.") The Fairy Godmother Department presents us with what the Quartermaster describes as "Boots, gum, thigh"; and there
has also been an issue of so-called fur jackets, in
which the Practical Joke Department has plainly
taken a hand. Most of these garments appear to
have been contributed by animals unknown to
zoölogy, or more probably by a syndicate thereof.
Corporal Mucklewame's costume gives him the
appearance of a St. Bernard dog with Astrakhan
fore legs. Sergeant Carfrae is attired in what
looks like the skin of Nana, the dog-nurse in
"Peter Pan." Private Nigg, an undersized youth

of bashful disposition, creeps forlornly about his
duties disguised as an imitation leopard. As he
passes by, facetious persons pull what is left of his
tail. Private Tosh, on being confronted with his
winter *trousseau*, observed bitterly —

"I jined the Airmy for tae be a sojer; but I doot
they must have pit me doon as a mountain goat!"

Still, though our variegated pelts cause us to re-
semble an unsuccessful compromise between Esau
and an Eskimo, they keep our bodies warm. We
wish we could say the same for our feet. On good
days we stand ankle-deep; on bad, we are occasionally over the knees. Thrice blessed then are
our Boots, Gum, Thigh, though even these cannot
altogether ward off frost-bite and chilblains.

Over the way, Brother Boche is having a bad
time of it: his trenches are in a worse state than
ours. Last night a plaintive voice cried out —

"Are you dere, Jock? Haf you whiskey? We
haf plenty water!"

Not bad for a Boche, the platoon decided.

There is no doubt that whatever the German
General Staff may think about the war and the
future, the German Infantry soldier is "fed-up."
His satiety takes the form of a craving for social
intercourse with the foe. In the small hours, when
the vigilance of the German N.C.O.'s is relaxed,
and the officers are probably in their dug-outs,
he makes rather pathetic overtures. We are frequently invited to come out and shake hands.
"Dis war will be ober the nineteen of nex' month!"
(Evidently the Kaiser has had another revela-
tion.) The other morning a German soldier, with

a wisp of something white in his hand, actually clambered out of the firing-trench and advanced towards our lines. The distance was barely seventy yards. No shot was fired, but you may be sure that safety-catches were hastily released. Suddenly, in the tense silence, the ambassador's nerve failed him. He bolted back, followed by a few desultory bullets. The reason for his sudden panic was never rightly ascertained, but the weight of public opinion inclined to the view that Mucklewame, who had momentarily exposed himself above the parapet, was responsible.

"I doot he thocht ye were a lion escapit from the Scottish Zoo!" explained a brother corporal, referring to his indignant colleague's new winter coat.

Here is another incident, with a different ending. At one point our line approaches to within fifteen yards of the Boche trenches. One wet and dismal dawn, as the battalion stood to arms in the neighbourhood of this delectable spot, there came a sudden shout from the enemy, and an outburst of rapid rifle fire. Almost simultaneously two breathless and unkempt figures tumbled over our parapet into the firing-trench. The fusillade died away.

To the extreme discomfort and shame of a respectable citizen of Bannockburn, one Private Buncle, the more hairy of the two visitors, upon recovering his feet, promptly flung his arms around his neck and kissed him on both cheeks. The outrage was repeated, by his companion, upon Private Nigg. At the same time both visitors

broke into a joyous chant of "Russky! Russky!"
They were escaped Russian prisoners.

When taken to Headquarters they explained
that they had been brought up to perform fatigue
work near the German trenches, and had seized
upon a quiet moment to slip into some convenient
undergrowth. Later, under cover of night, they
had made their way in the direction of the firing-
line, arriving just in time to make a dash before
daylight discovered them. You may imagine
their triumphal departure from our trenches —
loaded with cigarettes, chocolate, bully beef, and
other imperishable souvenirs.

We have had other visitors. One bright day a
Boche aeroplane made a reconnaissance of our
lines. It was a beautiful thing, white and birdlike.
But as its occupants were probably taking photographs of our most secret fastnesses, artistic appreciation was dimmed by righteous wrath —
wrath which turned to profound gratification
when a philistine British plane appeared in the
blue and engaged the glittering stranger in
battle. There was some very pretty aerial ma-
nœuvring, right over our heads, as the combatants swooped and circled for position. We could
hear their machine-guns pattering away; and
the volume of sound was increased by the distant
contributions of "Coughing Clara" — our latest
anti-aircraft gun, which appears to suffer from
chronic irritation of the mucous membrane.

Suddenly the German aeroplane gave a lurch;
then righted herself; then began to circle down,
making desperate efforts to cross the neutral line.

But the British airman headed her off. Next
moment she lurched again, and then took a "nose-
dive" straight into the British trenches. She fell
on open ground, a few hundred yards behind our
second line. The place had been a wilderness a
moment before; but the crowd which instantane-
ously sprang up round the wreck could not have
been less than two hundred strong. (One observes
the same uncanny phenomenon in London, when
a cab-horse falls down in a deserted street.) However, it melted away at the rebuke of the first officer who hurried to the spot, the process of dissolu-
tion being accelerated by several bursts of German shrapnel.

Both pilot and observer were dead. They had
made a gallant fight, and were buried the same
evening, with all honour, in the little cemetery,
alongside many who had once been their foes, but
were now peacefully neutral.

IV

The housing question in Belgium confronts us
with several novel problems. It is not so easy to
billet troops here, especially in the Salient, as in
France. Some of us live in huts, others in tents,
others in dug-outs. Others, more fortunate, are
loaded on to a fleet of motor-buses and whisked
off to more civilised dwellings many miles away.
These buses once plied for hire upon the streets of
London. Each bus is in charge of the identical
pair of cross-talk comedians who controlled its
destinies in more peaceful days. Strangely attired
in khaki and sheepskin, they salute officers with

cheerful *bonhomie*, and bellow to one another
throughout the journey the simple and primitive
jests of their previous incarnation, to the huge
delight of their fares.

The destination-boards and advertisements are
no more, for the buses are painted a neutral green
all over; but the conductor is always ready and
willing to tell you what his previous route was.

"That Daimler behind you, sir," he informs
you, "is one of the Number Nineteens. Set you
down at the top of Sloane Street many a time, I'll
be bound. Ernie" — this to the driver, along the
side of the bus — "you oughter have slowed
down when thet copper waved his little flag: he
was n't pleased with yer, ole son!" (The "copper" is a military mounted policeman, controlling
the traffic of a little town which lies on our way to
the trenches.) "This is a Number Eight, sir. No,
that dent in the staircase was n't done by no shell.
The ole girl got that through a skid up against a
lamp-post, one wet Saturday night in the Vaux-
hall Bridge Road. Dangerous place, London!"

We rattle through a brave little town, which is
"carrying on" in the face of paralysed trade and
periodical shelling. Soldiers abound. All are
muddy, but some are muddier than others. The
latter are going up to the trenches, the former are
coming back. Upon the walls, here and there, we
notice a gay poster advertising an entertainment
organised by certain Divisional troops, which is to
be given nightly throughout the week. At the
foot of the bill is printed in large capitals, A
HOOGE SUCCESS! We should like to send a

copy of that plucky document to Brother Boche.
He would not understand it, but it would annoy
him greatly.

Now we leave the town behind, and quicken
up along the open road — an interminable ribbon
of *pavé*, absolutely straight, and bordered upon
either side by what was once macadam, but is
now a quagmire a foot deep. Occasionally there
is a warning cry of "Wire!" and the outside fares
hurriedly bow from the waist, in order to avoid
having their throats cut by a telephone wire —
"Gunners, for a dollar!" surmises a strangled
voice — tightly stretched across the road between
two poplars. Occasionally, too, that indefatigable humorist, Ernie, directs his course beneath
some low-spreading branches, through which the
upper part of the bus crashes remorselessly, while
the passengers, lying sardine-wise upon the roof
uplift their voices in profane and bloodthirsty
chorus.

"Nothing like a bit o' fun on the way to the
trenches, boys! It may be the last you'll get!" is
the only apology which Ernie offers.

Presently our vehicle bumps across a nubbly
bridge, and enters what was once a fair city. It is
a walled city, like Chester, and is separated from
the surrounding country by a moat as wide as the
upper Thames. In days gone by those ramparts
and that moat could have held an army at bay —
and probably did, more than once. They have
done so yet again; but at what a cost!

We glide through the ancient gateway and

along the ghostly streets, and survey the crowning achievement of the cultured Boche. The great buildings — the Cathedral, the Cloth Hall — are jagged ruins. The fronts of the houses have long disappeared, leaving the interiors exposed to view, like a doll's house. Here is a street full of shops. That heap of splintered wardrobes and legless tables was once a furniture warehouse. That snug little corner house, with the tottering zinc counter and the twisted beer engine, is an obvious estaminet. You may observe the sign, "Aux Deux Amis," in dingy lettering over the doorway. Here is an oil-and-colour shop: you can still see the red ochre and white lead splashed about among the ruins.

In almost every house the ceilings of the upper floors have fallen in. Chairs, tables, and bedsteads hang precariously into the room below. Here and there a picture still adheres to the wall. From one of the bedposts flutters a tattered and diminutive garment of blue and white check — some little girl's frock. Where is that little girl now, we wonder; and has she got another frock?

One is struck above all things with the minute detail of the damage. You would say that a party of lunatics had been let loose on the city with coal-hammers: there is hardly a square yard of any surface which is not pierced, or splintered, or dented. The whole fabric of the place lies prostrate, under a shroud of broken bricks and broken plaster. The Hun has said in his majesty: "If you will not yield me this, the last city in the last corner of Belgium, I can at least see to it that

not one stone thereof remains upon another.
— So yah!"

Such is the appearance presented by the venerable and historic city of Ypres, after fifteen months of personal contact with the apostles of the new civilisation. Only the methodical and painstaking Boche could have reduced a town of such a size to such a state. Imagine Chester in a similar condition, and you may realise the number of shells which have fallen, and are still falling, into the stricken city.

But — the main point to observe is this. We are inside, and the Boche is outside! Fenced by a mighty crescent of prosaic trenches, themselves manned by paladins of an almost incredible stolidity, Ypres still points her broken fingers to the sky — shattered, silent, but inviolate still; and all owing to the obstinacy of a dull and unready nation which merely keeps faith and stands by its friends. Such an attitude of mind is incomprehensible to the Boche, and we are well content that it should be so.

II

I

THIS, according to our latest subaltern from home, is the title of a *revue* which is running in Town; but that is a mere coincidence. The entertainment to which I am now referring took place in Flanders, and the leading parts were assigned to distinguished members of "K (1)."

The scene was the Château de Grandbois, or some other kind of Bois; possibly Vert. Not that we called it that: we invariably referred to it afterwards as Hush Hall, for reasons which will be set forth in due course.

One morning, while sojourning in what Olympus humorously calls a rest-camp, — a collection of antiquated wigwams half submerged in a mud-flat, — we received the intelligence that we were to extricate ourselves forthwith, and take over a fresh sector of trenches. The news was doubly unwelcome, because, in the first place, it is always unpleasant to face the prospect of trenches of any kind; and secondly, to take over strange trenches in the dead of a winter night is an experience which borders upon nightmare — the hot-lobster-and-toasted-cheese variety.

The opening stages of this enterprise are almost ritualistic in their formality. First of all, the Brigade Staff which is coming in visits the Headquar-

ters of the Brigade which is going out — usually a
château or farm somewhere in rear of the trenches
— and makes the preliminary arrangements. After that the Commanding Officers and Company
Commanders of the incoming battalions visit
their own particular section of the line. They are
shown over the premises by the outgoing tenants,
who make little or no attempt to conceal their
satisfaction at the expiration of their lease. The
Colonels and the Captains then return to camp,
with depressing tales of crumbling parapets, noisome dug-outs, and positions open to enfilade.

On the day of the relief various advance parties
go up, keeping under the lee of hedges and em-
bankments, and marching in single file. (At least,
that is what they are supposed to do. If not ruth-
lessly shepherded, they will advance in fours along
the skyline.) Having arrived, they take over such
positions as can be relieved by daylight in comparative safety. They also take over trench-
stores, and exchange trench-gossip. The latter is
a fearsome and uncanny thing. It usually begins
life at the "refilling point," where the A.S.C.
motor-lorries dump down next day's rations, and
the regimental transport picks them up.

An A.S.C. Sergeant mentions casually to a regimental Quartermaster that he has heard it said at
the Supply Dépôt that heavy firing has been going
on in the Channel. The Quartermaster, on returning to the Transport Lines, observes to his Quartermaster-Sergeant that the German Fleet has
come out at last. The Quartermaster-Sergeant,
when he meets the ration parties behind the lines

that night, announces to a platoon Sergeant that we have won a great naval victory. The platoon Sergeant, who is suffering from trench feet and is a constant reader of a certain pessimistic halfpenny journal, replies gloomily: "We'll have had heavy losses oorselves, too, I doot!" This observation is overheard by various members of the ration party. By midnight several hundred yards of the firing-line know for a fact that there has been a naval disaster of the first magnitude off the coast of a place which every one calls Gally Polly, and that the whole of our Division are to be transferred forthwith to the Near East to stem the tide of calamity.

Still, we must have *something* to chat about.

Meanwhile Brigade Majors and Adjutants, holding a stumpy pencil in one hand and a burning brow in the other, are composing Operation Orders which shall effect the relief, without —

(1) Leaving some detail — the bombers, or the snipers, or the sock-driers, or the pea-soup experts — unrelieved altogether.

(2) Causing relievers and relieved to meet violently together in some constricted fairway.

(3) Trespassing into some other Brigade Area. (This is far more foolhardy than to wander into the German lines.)

(4) Getting shelled.

Pitfall Number One is avoided by keeping a permanent and handy list of "all the people who do funny things on their own" (as the vulgar throng call the "specialists"), and checking it carefully before issuing Orders.

Number Two is dealt with by issuing a strict time-table, which might possibly be adhered to by a well-drilled flock of archangels, in broad daylight, upon good roads, and under peace conditions.

Number Three is provided for by copious and complicated map references.

Number Four is left to Providence — and is usually the best-conducted feature of the excursion.

Under cover of night the Battalion sets out, in comparatively small parties. They form a strange procession. The men wear their trench-costume — thigh-boots (which do not go well with a kilt), variegated coats of skins, and woollen nightcaps. Stuffed under their belts and through their packs they carry newspapers, broken staves for firewood, parcels from home, and sandbags loaded with mysterious comforts. A dilapidated parrot and a few goats are all that is required to complete the picture of Robinson Crusoe changing camp.

Progress is not easy. It is a pitch-black night. By day, this road (and all the countryside) is a wilderness: nothing more innocent ever presented itself to the eye of an inquisitive aeroplane. But after nightfall it is packed with troops and transport, and not a light is shown. If you can imagine what the Mansion House crossing would be like if called upon to sustain its midday traffic at midnight — the Mansion House crossing entirely unilluminated, paved with twelve inches of liquid mud, intersected by narrow strips of *pavé*, and liberally pitted with "crump-holes" — you may derive some faint idea of the state of things at a busy road-junction lying behind the trenches.

Until reaching what is facetiously termed "the shell area" — as if any spot in this benighted district were not a shell area — the troops plod along in fours at the right of the road. If they can achieve two miles an hour, they do well. At any moment they may be called upon to halt, and crowd into the roadside,, while a transport-train passes carrying rations, and coke, and what is called "R.E. material" — this may be anything from a bag of nails to steel girders nine feet long— up to the firing-line. When this procession, consisting of a dozen limbered waggons, drawn by four mules and headed by a profane person on horseback — the Transport Officer — has rumbled past, the Company, which has been standing respectfully in the ditch, enjoying a refreshing shower-bath of mud and hoping that none of the steel girders are projecting from the limber more than a yard or two, sets out once more upon its way — only to take hasty cover again as sounds of fresh and more animated traffic are heard approaching from the opposite direction. There is no mistaking the nature of this cavalcade: the long vista of glowing cigarette-ends tells an unmistakable tale. These are artillery waggons, returning empty from replenishing the batteries; scattering homely jests like hail, and proceeding, wherever possible, at a hand-gallop. He is a cheery soul, the R.A. driver, but his interpretation of the rules of the road requires drastic revision.

Sometimes an axle breaks, or a waggon side-
slips off the *pavé* into the morass reserved for
infantry, and overturns. The result is a block,
which promptly extends forward and back for a
couple of miles. A peculiarly British chorus of
inquiry and remonstrance — a blend of biting
sarcasm and blasphemous humour — surges up
and down the line; until plunging mules are un-
yoked, and the offending vehicle man-handled out
of sight into the inky blackness by the roadside;
or, in extreme cases, is annihilated with axes.
Everything has to make way for a ration train.
To crown all, it is more than likely that the calm-
ness and smooth working of the proceedings will
be assisted by a burst of shrapnel overhead. It is a
most amazing scrimmage altogether. One of those
members of His Majesty's Opposition who are
doing so much at present to save our country from
destruction, by kindly pointing out the mistakes
of the British Government and the British Army,
would refer to the whole scene as a pandemonium
of mismanagement and ineptitude. And yet,
though the scene is enacted night after night
without a break, there is hardly a case on record
of the transport being surprised upon these roads
by the coming of daylight, and none whatever
of the rations and ammunition failing to get
through.

It is difficult to imagine that Brother Boche,
who on the other side of that ring of star-shells is
conducting a precisely similar undertaking, is
able, with all his perfect organisation and cast-
iron methods, to achieve a result in any way su-

perior to that which Thomas Atkins reaches by
rule of thumb and sheer force of character.

At length the draggled Company worms its
way through the press to the fringe of the shell-
area, beyond which no transport may pass. The
distance of this point from the trenches varies
considerably, and depends largely upon the ca-
price of the Boche. On this occasion, however,
we still have a mile or two to go — across country
now, in single file, at the heels of a guide from the
battalion which we are relieving.

Guides may be divided into two classes —

(1) Guides who do not know the way, and say
so at the outset.

(2) Guides who do not know the way, but leave
it to you to discover the fact.

There are no other kinds of guides.

The pace is down to a mile an hour now, except
in the case of men in the tail of the line, who are
running rapidly. It is a curious but quite inexpli-
cable fact that if you set a hundred men to march
in single file in the dark, though the leading man
may be crawling like a tortoise, the last man is
compelled to proceed at a profane double if he is
to avoid being left behind and lost.

Still, everybody gets there somehow, and in due
course the various Company Commanders are
enabled to telephone to their respective Battalion
Headquarters the information that the Relief is
completed. For this relief, much thanks!

After that the outgoing Battalion files slowly
out, and the newcomers are left gloomily con-

templating their new abiding-place, and observing —

"I wonder if there is *any* Division in the whole blessed Expeditionary Force, besides ours, which ever does a single damn thing to keep its trenches in repair!"

II

All of which brings us back to Hush Hall, where the Headquarters of the outgoing Brigade are handing over to their successors.

Hush Hall, or the Château de Quelquechose, is a modern country house, and once stood up white and gleaming in all its brave finery of stucco, conservatories, and ornamental lake, amid a pleasant wood not far from a main road. It is such a house as you might find round about Guildford or Hindhead. There are many in this fair countryside, but few are inhabited now, and none by their rightful owners. They are all marked on the map, and the Boche gunners are assiduous map-readers. Hush Hall has got off comparatively lightly. It is still habitable, and well furnished. The roof is demolished upon the side most exposed to the enemy, and many of the trees in the surrounding wood are broken and splintered by shrapnel. Still, provided the weather remains passable, one can live there. Upon the danger-side the windows are closed and shuttered. Weeds grow apace in the garden. No smoke emerges from the chimneys. (If it does, the Mess Corporal hears about it from the Staff Captain.) A few strands of barbed wire obstruct the passage of those careless or adventurous persons who may desire to explore the forbidden side of the house. The front door is bolted and barred: visitors, after approaching stealthily along the lee of a hedge, like travellers of dubious *bona fides* on a Sunday afternoon, enter unobtrusively by the back door, which is situated on the blind side of the château. Their path thereto is beset by imploring notices like the following: —

> THE SLIGHTEST MOVEMENT DRAWS SHELL
> FIRE. KEEP CLOSE TO THE HEDGE

A later hand has added the following moving postscript: —

> WE LIVE HERE. YOU DON'T!

It was the Staff Captain who was responsible for the rechristening of the establishment.

"What sort of place is this new palace we are going to doss in?" inquired the Machine-Gun Officer, when the Staff Captain returned from his preliminary visit.

The Staff Captain, who was a man of a few words, replied —

"It's the sort of shanty where everybody goes about in felt slippers, saying 'Hush!'"

Brigade Headquarters — this means the Brigadier, the Brigade Major, the Staff Captain, the

Machine-Gun Officer, the Signal Officer, mayhap a Padre and a Liaison Officer, accompanied by a mixed multitude of clerks, telegraphists, and scullions — arrived safely at their new quarters under cover of night, and were hospitably received by the outgoing tenants, who had finished their evening meal and were girded up for departure. In fact, the Machine-Gun Officer, Liaison Officer, and Padre had already gone, leaving their seniors to hold the fort till the last. The Signal Officer was down in the cellar, handing over ohms, ampères, short-circuits, and other mysterious trench-stores to his "opposite number."

Upon these occasions there is usually a good deal of time to fill in between the arrival of the new brooms and the departure of the old. This period of waiting may be likened to that somewhat anxious interval with which frequenters of race-courses are familiar, between the finish of the race and the announcement of the "All Right!" The outgoing Headquarters are waiting for the magic words — "Relief Complete!" Until that message comes over the buzzer, the period of tension endures. The main point of difference is that the gentleman who has staked his fortune on the legs of a horse has only to wait a few minutes for the confirmation of his hopes; while a Brigadier, whose bedtime (or even breakfast-time) is at the mercy of an errant platoon, may have to sit up all night.

"Sit down and make yourselves comfortable," said A Brigade to X Brigade.

X Brigade complied, and having been furnished

with refreshment, led off with the inevitable
question —

"Does one — er — get shelled much here?"

There was a reassuring coo from A Brigade.

"Oh, no. This is a very healthy spot. One has
to be careful, of course. No movement, or fires, or
anything of that kind. A sentry or two, to warn
people against approaching over the open by day,
and you'll be as cooshie as anything!" ("Cooshie"
is the latest word here. That and "crump.")

"I ought to warn you of one thing," said the
Brigadier. "Owing to the surrounding woods,
sound is most deceptive here. You will hear shell-
bursts which appear quite close, when in reality
they are quite a distance away. That, for instance!" — as a shell exploded apparently just
outside the window. "That little fellow is a
couple of hundred yards away, in the corner of
the wood. The Boche has been groping about
there for a battery for the last two days."

"Is the battery there?" inquired a voice.

"No; it is farther east. But there is a Gunner's
Mess about two hundred yards from here, in
that house which you passed on the way up."

"Oh!" observed X Brigade.

Gunners are peculiar people. When profes-
sionally engaged, no men could be more retiring.
They screen their operations from the public gaze
with the utmost severity, shrouding batteries in
screens of foliage and other rustic disguises. If a
layman strays anywhere near one of these arbo-
real retreats, a gunner thrusts out a visage en-
flamed with righteous wrath, and curses him for

giving the position away. But in his hours of relaxation the gunner is a different being. He billets himself in a house with plenty of windows: he illuminates all these by night, and hangs washing therefrom by day. When inclined for exercise, he goes for a promenade across an open space labelled — "Not to be used by troops by daylight." Therefore, despite his technical excellence and superb courage, he is an uncomfortable neighbour for establishments like Hush Hall.

In this respect he offers a curious contrast to the Sapper. Off duty, the Sapper is the most unobtrusive of men — a cave-man, in fact. He burrows deep into the earth, or the side of a hill, and having secured the roof of this cavern against direct hits by ingenious contrivances of his own manufacture, constructs a suite of furniture of a solid and enduring pattern, and lives the life of a comfortable recluse. But when engaged in the pursuit of his calling, the Sapper is the least retiring of men. The immemorial tradition of the great Corps to which he belongs has ordained that no fire, however fierce, must be allowed to interfere with a Sapper in the execution of his duty. This rule is usually interpreted by the Sapper to mean that you must not perform your allotted task under cover when it is possible to do so under fire. To this is added, as a rider, that in the absence of an adequate supply of fire, you must draw fire. So the Sapper walks cheerfully about on the tops of parapets, hugging large and conspicuous pieces of timber, or clashing together sheets of corrugated iron, as happy as a king.

"You will find this house quite snug," continued the Brigadier. "The eastern suite is to be
avoided, because there is no roof there; and if it
rains outside for a day, it rains in the best bedroom for a week. There is a big kitchen in the
basement, with a capital range. That's all, I
think. The chief thing to avoid is movement of
any kind. The leaves are coming off the trees
now —"

At this moment an orderly entered the room
with a pink telegraph message.

"Relief complete, sir!" announced the Brigade
Major, reading it.

"Good work!" replied both Brigadiers, looking
at their watches simultaneously, "considering the
state of the country." The Brigadier of "A" rose
to his feet.

"Now we can pass along quietly," he said.
"Good luck to you. By the way, take care of
Edgar, won't you? Any little attention which you
can show him will be greatly appreciated."

"Who is Edgar?"

"Oh, I thought the Staff Captain would have
told you. Edgar is the swan — the last of his race,
I'm afraid, so far as this place is concerned. He
lives on the lake, and usually comes ashore to
draw his rations about lunch-time. He is inclined
to be stand-offish on one side, as he has only one
eye; but he is most affable on the other. Well,
now to find our horses!"

As the three officers departed down the back-
door steps, a hesitating voice followed them —

"H'm! Is there any place where one can go —

a cellar, or any old spot of that kind — just in
case we are —"

"Bless you, you'll be all right!" was the cheery
reply. (The outgoing Brigade is always excessively cheery.) "But there are dug-outs over
there — in the garden. They have n't been occupied for some months, so you may find them a bit
ratty. You won't require them, though. Good-
night!"

III

Whizz! Boom! Bang! Crash! Wump!

"It's just as well," mused the Brigade Major,
turning in his sleep about three o'clock the following morning, "that they warned us about the deceptive sound of the shelling here. One would
almost imagine that it was quite close. . . . That
last one was heavy stuff: it shook the whole place!
. . . This is a topping mattress: it would be rotten
having to take to the woods again after getting
into really cooshie quarters at last. . . . There
they go again!" as a renewed tempest of shells
rent the silence of night. "That old battery must
be getting it in the neck! . . . Hallo, I could have
sworn something hit the roof that time! A loose
slate, I expect! Anyhow . . ."

The Brigade Major, who had had a very long
day, turned over and went to sleep again.

IV

The next morning, a Sunday, broke bright and
clear. Contrary to his usual habit, the Brigade
Major took a stroll in the garden before breakfast.

The first object which caught his eye, as he came down the back-door steps, was the figure of the Staff Captain, brooding pensively over a large crater, close to the hedge. The Brigade Major joined him.

"I wonder if that was there yesterday!" he observed, referring to the crater.

"Could n't have been," growled the Staff Captain. "We walked to the house along this very hedge. No craters then!"

"True!" agreed the Brigade Major amiably. He turned and surveyed the garden. "That lawn looks a bit of a golf course. What lovely bunkers!"

"They appear to be quite new, too," remarked the Staff Captain thoughtfully. "Come to breakfast!"

On their way back they found the Brigadier, the Machine-Gun Officer, and the Padre, gazing silently upward.

"I wonder when that corner of the house got knocked off," the M.G.O. was observing.

"Fairly recently, I should say," replied the Brigadier.

"Those marks beside your bedroom window, sir, — they look pretty fresh!" interpolated the Padre, a sincere but somewhat tactless Christian.

Brigade Headquarters regarded one another with dubious smiles.

"I *wonder*," began a tentative voice, "if those fellows last night were indulging in a leg-pull — what is called in this country a *tire-jambe* — when they assured us —"

Whoo-oo-oo-oo-ump!

A shell came shrieking over the tree-tops, and
fell with a tremendous splash into the geometrical
centre of the lake, fifty yards away.

For the next two hours, shrapnel, "whizz-
bangs," "Silent Susies," and other explosive wild-
fowl raged round the walls of Hush Hall. The
inhabitants thereof, some twenty persons in all,
were gathered in various apartments on the lee
side.

"It is still possible," remarked the Brigadier,
lighting his pipe, "that they are not aiming at us.
However, it is just as inconvenient to be buried
by accident as by design. As soon as the first
direct hit is registered upon this imposing fabric,
we will retire to the dug-outs. Send word to the
kitchen that every one is to be ready to clear out
of the house when necessary."

Next moment there came a resounding crash,
easily audible above the tornado raging in the
garden, followed by the sound of splintering glass.
Hush Hall rocked. The Mess waiter appeared.

"A shell has just came in through the dining-
room window, sirr," he informed the Mess President, "and broke three of they new cups!"

"How tiresome!" said the Brigadier. "Dug-
outs, everybody!"

V

There were no casualties, which was rather
miraculous. Late in the afternoon Brigade Headquarters ventured upon another stroll in the gar-

den. The tumult had ceased, and the setting Sabbath sun glowed peacefully upon the battered countenance of Hush Hall. The damage was not very extensive, for the house was stoutly built. Still, two bedrooms, recently occupied, were a wreck of broken glass and splintered plaster, while the gravel outside was littered with lead sheeting and twisted chimney-cans. The shell which had aroused the indignation of the Mess waiter by entering the dining-room window, had in reality hit the ground directly beneath it. Six feet higher, and the Brigadier's order to clear the house would have been entirely superfluous.

The Brigade Major and the Staff Captain surveyed the unruffled surface of the lake — a haunt of ancient peace in the rays of the setting sun. Upon the bosom thereof floated a single, majestic, one-eyed swan, performing intricate toilet exercises. It was Edgar.

"He must have a darned good dug-out somewhere!" observed the Brigade Major enviously.

III

I

HUSH HALL having become an even less desirable place of residence than had hitherto been thought possible, Headquarters very sensibly sent for their invaluable friends, Box and Cox, of the Royal Engineers, and requested that they would proceed to make the place proof against shells and weather, forthwith, if not sooner.

Those phlegmatic experts made a thorough investigation of the resources of the establishment, and departed mysteriously, after the fashion of the common plumber of civilisation, into space. Three days later they returned, accompanied by a horde of acolytes, who, with characteristic contempt for the pathetic appeals upon the notice-boards, proceeded to dump down lumber, sand-bags, and corrugated iron roofing in the most exposed portions of the garden.

This done, some set out to shore up the ceilings of the basement with mighty battens of wood, and to convert that region into a nest of cunningly devised bedrooms. Others reinforced the flooring above with a layer of earth and brick rubble three feet deep. On the top of all this they relaid not only the original floor, but eke the carpet.

"The only difference from before, sir," explained Box to the admiring Staff Captain, "is

that people will have to walk up three steps to get
into the dining-room now, instead of going in on
the level."

"I wonder what the Marquise de Chilquichose
will think of it all when she returns to her ancestral home," mused the Staff Captain.

"If anything," maintained the invincible Box,
"we have improved it for her. For example, she
can now light the chandelier without standing on
a chair — without getting up from table, in fact!
However, to resume. The fireplace, you will observe, has not been touched. I have left a sort of
well in the floor all round it, lined with some stuff
I found in Mademoiselle's room. At least," added
Box coyly, "I think it must have been Mademoiselle's room! You can sit in the well every evening
after supper. The walls of this room" — prod-
ding the same — "are lined with sandbags, covered with tapestry. Pretty artistic — what?"

"Extremely," agreed the Staff Captain. "You
will excuse my raising the point, I know, but can
the apartment now be regarded as shell-proof?"

"Against everything but a direct hit. I
would n't advise you to sleep on this floor much,
but you could have your meals here all right.
Then, if the Boche starts putting over heavy
stuff, you can pop down into the basement and
have your dessert in bed. You'll be absolutely
safe there. In fact, the more the house tumbles
down the safer you will be. It will only make your
protection shell thicker. So if you hear heavy
thuds overhead, don't be alarmed!"

"I won't," promised the Staff Captain. "I

shall lie in bed, drinking a nice hot cup of tea, and
wondering whether the last crash was the kitchen
chimney, or only the drawing-room piano coming
down another storey. Now show me my room."

"We have had to put you in the larder," explained Box apologetically, as he steered his guest
through a forest of struts with an electric torch.
"At least, I think it's the larder: it has a sort of
meaty smell. The General is in the dairy — a
lovely little suite, with white tiles. The Brigade
Major has the scullery: it has a sink, so is practically as good as a flat in Park Place. I have run
up cubicles for the others in the kitchen. Here is
your little cot. It is only six feet by four, but you
can dress in the garden."

"It's a *sweet* little nest, dear!" replied the Staff
Captain, quite hypnotised by this time. "I'll just
get my maid to put me into something loose, and
then I'll run along to your room, and we'll have a
nice cosy gossip together before dinner!"

In due course we removed our effects from the
tottering and rat-ridden dug-outs in which we had
taken sanctuary during the shelling, and prepared
to settle down for the winter in our new quarters.

"We might be *very* much worse off!" we observed the first evening, listening to the comfortably muffled sounds of shells overhead.

And we were right. Three days later we received an intimation from the Practical Joke Department that we were to evacuate our present
sector of trenches (including Hush Hall) forthwith, and occupy another part of the line.

In all Sports, Winter and Summer, the supremacy of the Practical Joke Department is unchallenged.

II

Meanwhile, up in the trenches, the combatants are beguiling the time in their several ways.

Let us take the reserve line first — the lair of Battalion Headquarters and its appurtenances. Much of our time here, as elsewhere, is occupied in unostentatious retirement to our dug-outs, to avoid the effects of a bombardment. But a good amount — an increasing amount — of it is devoted to the contemplation of our own shells bursting over the Boche trenches. Gone are the days during which we used to sit close and "stick it out," consoling ourselves with the vague hope that by the end of the week our gunners might possibly have garnered sufficient ammunition to justify a few brief hours' retaliation. The boot is on the other leg now. For every Boche battery that opens on us, two or three of ours thunder back a reply — and that without any delays other than those incidental to the use of that maddening instrument, the field-telephone. During the past six months neither side has been able to boast much in the way of ground actually gained; but the moral ascendancy — the initiative — the offensive — call it what you will — has changed hands; and no one knows it better than the Boche. We are the attacking party now.

The trenches in this country are not arranged with such geometric precision as in France. For

instance, the reserve line is not always connected
with the firing-lines by a communication-trench.
Those persons whose duty it is to pay daily visits
to the fire-trenches — Battalion Commanders,
Gunner and Sapper officers, an occasional Staff
Officer, and an occasional most devoted Padre —
perform the journey as best they may. Sometimes
they skirt a wood or hedge, sometimes they keep
under the lee of an embankment, sometimes they
proceed across the open, with the stealthy caution
of persons playing musical chairs, ready to sit
down in the nearest shell-crater the moment the
music — in the form of a visitation of "whizz-
bangs" — strikes up.

It is difficult to say which kind of weather is
least favourable to this enterprise. On sunny days
one's movements are visible to Boche observers
upon distant summits; while on foggy days the
Boche gunners, being able to see nothing at all,
amuse themselves by generous and unexpected
contributions of shrapnel in all directions. Stormy
weather is particularly unpleasant, for the noise of
the wind in the trees makes it difficult to hear the
shell approaching. Days of heavy rain are the
most desirable on the whole, for then the gunners
are too busy bailing out their gun-pits to worry
their heads over adventurous pedestrians. One
learns, also, to mark down and avoid particular
danger-spots. For instance, the southeast corner
of that wood, where a reserve company are dug in,
is visited by "Silent Susans" for about five minutes each noontide: it is therefore advisable to select some other hour for one's daily visit. (Silent

Susan, by the way, is not a desirable member of
the sex. Owing to her intensely high velocity she
arrives overhead without a sound, and then bursts
with a perfectly stunning detonation and a shower
of small shrapnel bullets.) There is a fixed rifle-
battery, too, which fires all day long, a shot at a
time, down the main street of the ruined and deserted village named Vrjoozlehem, through which
one must pass on the way to the front-line
trenches. Therefore in negotiating this delectable spot, one shapes a laborious course through a
series of back yards and garden-plots, littered
with broken furniture and brick rubble, allowing
the rifle-bullets the undisputed use of the street.

The mention of Vrjoozlehem — that is not its
real name, but a simplified form of it — brings to
our notice the wholesale and whole-hearted fashion in which the British Army has taken Belgian
institutions under its wing. Nomenclature, for
instance. In France we make no attempt to interfere with this: we content ourselves with devising
a pronounceable variation of the existing name.
For example, if a road is called La Rue de Bois,
we simply call it "Roodiboys," and leave it at
that. On the same principle, Etaples is modified
to "Eatables," and Sailly-la-Bourse to "Sally
Booze." But in Belgium more drastic procedure is
required. A Scotsman is accustomed to pronounc-
ing difficult names, but even he is unable to con-
tend with words composed almost entirely of the
letters j, z, and v. So our resourceful Ordnance
Department has issued maps — admirable maps
— upon which the outstanding features of the

landscape are marked in plain figures. But instead of printing the original place-names, they
put "Moated Grange," or "Clapham Junction," or "Dead Dog Farm," which simplifies
matters beyond all possibility of error. (The system was once responsible, though, for an unjust if
unintentional aspersion upon the character of a
worthy man. The C.O. of a certain battalion had
occasion to complain to those above him of the
remissness of one of his chaplains. "He's a lazy
beggar, sir," he said. "Over and over again I have
told him to come up and show himself in the
front-line trenches, but he never seems to be able
to get past Leicester Square!")

The naming of the trenches themselves has
been left largely to local enterprise. An observant
person can tell, by a study of the numerous name-
boards, which of his countrymen have been occupying the line during the past six months.
"Grainger Street" and "Jesmond Dene" give
direct evidence of "Canny N'castle." "Sher-
wood Avenue" and "Notts Forest" have a Midland flavour. Lastly, no great mental effort is
required to decide who labelled two communication trenches "The Gorbals" and "Coocaddens"
respectively!

Some names have obviously been bestowed by
officers, as "Sackville Street," "The Albany,"
and "Burlington Arcade" denote. "Pinch-Gut"
and "Crab-Crawl" speak for themselves. So does
"Vermin Villa." Other localities, again, have
obviously been labelled by persons endowed with
a nice gift of irony. "Sanctuary Wood" is the last

place on earth where any one would dream of taking sanctuary; while "Lovers' Walk," which
bounds it, is the scene of almost daily expositions
of the choicest brand of Boche "hate."

And so on. But one day, when the War is over,
and this mighty trench-line is thrown open to the
disciples of the excellent Mr. Cook — as undoubtedly it will be — care should be taken that these
street-names are preserved and perpetuated. It
would be impossible to select a more characteristic
and fitting memorial to the brave hearts who constructed them — too many of whom are sleeping
their last sleep within a few yards of their own
cheerful handiwork.

III

After this digression we at length reach the
firing-line. It is quite unlike anything of its kind
that we have hitherto encountered. It is situated
in what was once a thick wood. Two fairly well-
defined trenches run through the undergrowth,
from which the sentries of either side have been
keeping relentless watch upon one another, night
and day, for many months. The wood itself is a
mere forest of poles: hardly a branch, and not a
twig, has been spared by the shrapnel. In the no-
man's-land between the trenches the poles have
been reduced to mere stumps a few inches high.

It is behind the firing-trench that the most
unconventional scene presents itself. Strictly
speaking, there ought to be — and generally is —
a support-line some seventy yards in rear of the
first. This should be occupied by all troops not

required in the firing-trench. But the trench is
empty — which is not altogether surprising, considering that it is half-full of water. Its rightful
occupants are scattered through the wood behind
— in dug-outs, in redoubts, or *en plein air* —
cooking, washing, or repairing their residences.
The whole scene suggests a gipsy encampment
rather than a fortified post. A hundred yards
away, through the trees, you can plainly discern
the Boche firing-trench, and the Boche in that
trench can discern you: yet never a shot comes.
It is true that bullets are humming through the air
and glancing off trees, but these are mostly due
to the enterprise of distant machine-guns and
rifle-batteries, firing from some position well
adapted for enfilade. Frontal fire there is little or
none. In the front-line trenches, at least, Brother
Boche has had enough of it. His motto now is,
"Live and let live!" In fact, he frequently makes
plaintive statements to that effect in the silence
of night.

You might think, then, that life in Willow
Grove would be a tranquil affair. But if you look
up among the few remaining branches of that tall
tree in the centre of the wood, you may notice
shreds of some material flapping in the breeze.
Those are sandbags — or were. Last night, within
the space of one hour, seventy-three shells fell into
this wood, and the first of them registered a direct
hit upon the dug-out of which those sandbags
formed part. There were eight men in that dug-
out. The telephone-wires were broken in the first
few minutes, and there was some delay before

word could be transmitted back to Headquarters. Then our big guns far in rear spoke out, until the enemy's batteries (probably in response to an urgent appeal from their own front line) ceased firing. Thereupon "A" Company, who at Bobby Little's behest had taken immediate cover in the water-logged support-trench, returned stolidly to their dug-outs in Willow Grove. Death, when he makes the mistake of raiding your premises every day, loses most of his terrors and becomes a bit of a bore.

This morning the Company presents its normal appearance: its numbers have been reduced by eight — *c'est tout !* It may be some one else's turn to-morrow, but after all, that is what we are here for. Anyhow, we are keeping the Boches out of "Wipers," and a bit over. So we stretch our legs in the wood, and keep the flooded trench for the next emergency.

Let us approach a group of four which is squatting sociably round a small and inadequate fire of twigs, upon which four mess-tins are simmering. The quartette consists of Privates Cosh and Tosh, together with Privates Buncle and Nigg, preparing their midday meal.

"Tak' off your damp chup, Jimmy," suggested Tosh to Buncle, who was officiating as stoker. "Ye mind what the Captain said aboot smoke?"

"It wasna the Captain: it was the Officer," rejoined Buncle cantankerously.

(It may here be explained, at the risk of another digression, that no length of association or degree of intimacy will render the average British

soldier familiar with the names of his officers. The
Colonel is "The C.O."; the Second in Command
is "The Major"; your Company Commander is
"The Captain," and your Platoon Commander
"The Officer." As for all others of commissioned
rank in the regiment, some twenty-four in all,
they are as nought. With the exception of the
Quartermaster, in whose shoes each member of
the rank and file hopes one day to stand, they
simply do not exist.)

"Onyway," pursued the careful Tosh, "he said
that if any smoke was shown, all fires was tae be
pitten oot. So mind and see no' to get a cauld
dinner for us all, Jimmy!"

"Cauld or het," retorted the gentleman addressed, "it's little dinner I'll be gettin' this day!
And ye ken fine why!" he added darkly.

Private Tosh removed a cigarette from his
lower lip and sighed patiently.

"For the last time," he announced, with the air
of a righteous man suffering long, "I did not lay
ma hand on your dirrty wee bit ham!"

"Maybe," countered the bereaved Buncle
swiftly, "you did not lay your hand upon it; but
you had it tae your breakfast for all that, Davie!"

"I never pit ma hand on it!" repeated Tosh
doggedly.

"No? Then I doot you gave it a bit kick with
your foot," replied the inflexible Buncle.

"Or got some other body tae luft it for him!"
suggested Private Nigg, looking hard at Tosh's
habitual accomplice, Cosh.

"I had it pitten in an auld envelope from

hame, addressed with my name," continued the mourner. "It couldna hae got oot o' that by accident!"

"Weel," interposed Cosh, with forced geniality, "it's no a thing tae argie-bargie aboot. Whatever body lufted it, it's awa' by this time. It's a fine day, boys!"

This flagrant attempt to raise the conversation to a less controversial plane met with no encouragement. Private Buncle, refusing to be appeased, replied sarcastically —

"Aye, is it? And it was a fine nicht last nicht, especially when the shellin' was gaun on! Especially in number seeven dug-oot!"

There was a short silence. Number seven dug-out was no more, and five of its late occupants were now lying under their waterproof sheets, not a hundred yards away, waiting for a Padre. Presently, however, the pacific Cosh, who in his hours of leisure was addicted to mild philosophical rumination, gave a fresh turn to the conversation.

"Mphm!" he observed thoughtfully. "They say that in a war every man has a bullet waiting for him some place or other, with his name on it! Sooner or later, he gets it. Aye! Mphm!" He sucked his teeth reflectively, and glanced towards the Field Ambulance. "Sooner or later!"

"What for would he pit his name on it, Wully?" inquired Nigg, who was not very quick at grasping allusions.

"He wouldna pit on the name himself," explained the philosopher. "What I mean is, there's a bullet for each one of us somewhere over there"

— he jerked his head eastward — "in a Gairman
pooch."

"What way could a Gairman pit my name on
a bullet?" demanded Nigg triumphantly. "He
doesna ken it!"

"Man," exclaimed Cosh, shedding some of his
philosophic calm, "can ye no unnerstand that
what I telled ye was jist a mainner of speakin'?
When I said that a man's name was on a bullet, I
didna mean that it was *written* there."

"Then what the hell *did* ye mean?" inquired
the mystified disciple — not altogether unreasonably.

Private Tosh made a misguided but well-
meaning attempt to straighten out the conversation.

"He means, Sandy," he explained in a soothing
voice, "that the name was just stampit on the
bullet. Like — like — like an identity disc!" he
added brilliantly.

The philosopher clutched his temples with both
hands.

"I dinna mean onything o' the kind," he
roared. "What I intend tae imply is *this*, Sandy
Nigg. Some place over there there is a bullet in a
Gairman's pooch, and one day that bullet will
find its way intil your insides as sure as if your
name was written on it! *That's* what I meant.
Jist a mainner of speakin'. Dae ye unnerstand me
the noo?"

But it was the injured Buncle who replied —
like a lightning-flash.

"Never you fear, Sandy, boy!" he proclaimed

to his perturbed ally. "That bullet has no' gotten
your length yet. Maybe it never wull. There's
mony a thing in this worrld with one man's name
on it that finds its way intil the inside of some
other man." He fixed Tosh with a relentless eye.
"A bit ham, for instance!"

It was a knock-out blow.

"For ony sake," muttered the now demoralised
Tosh, "drop the subject, and I'll gie ye a bit ham
o' ma ain! There's just time tae cook it —"

"What kin' o' a fire is this?"

A cold shadow fell upon the group as a substan-
tial presence inserted itself between the debaters
and the wintry sunshine. Corporal Mucklewame
was speaking, in his new and awful official voice,
pointing an accusing finger at the fire, which,
neglected in the ardour of discussion, was smoking
furiously.

"Did you wish the hale wood tae be shelled?"
continued Mucklewame sarcastically. "Put oot
the fire at once, or I'll need tae bring ye all before
the Officer. It is a cauld dinner ye'll get, and
ye'll deserve it! "

IV

In the fire-trench — or perhaps it would be
more correct to call it the water-trench — life
may be short, and is seldom merry; but it is not
often dull. For one thing, we are never idle.

A Boche trench-mortar knocks down several
yards of your parapet. Straightway your machine-
gunners are called up, to cover the gap until darkness falls and the gaping wound can be stanched

with fresh sandbags. A mine has been exploded
upon your front, leaving a crater into which pred-
atory Boches will certainly creep at night. You
summon a *posse* of bombers to occupy the cavity
and discourage any such enterprise. The heavens
open, and there is a sudden deluge. Immediately
it is a case of all hands to the trench-pump! A
better plan, if you have the advantage of ground,
is to cut a culvert under the parapet and pass the
inundation on to a more deserving quarter. In
any case you ne d never lack healthful exercise.

While upon the subject of mines, we may note
that this branch of military industry has expanded of late to most unpleasant dimensions.
The Boche began it, of course — he always initi-
ates these undesirable pastimes, — and now we
have followed his lead and caught him up.

To the ordinary mortal, to become a blind
groper amid the dark places of the earth, in search
of a foe whom it is almost certain death to encounter there, seems perhaps the most idiotic of
all the idiotic careers open to those who are idiotic
enough to engage in modern warfare. However,
many of us are as much at home below ground as
above it. In most peaceful times we were accustomed to spend eight hours a day there, lying up
against the "face" in a tunnel perhaps four feet
high, and wielding a pick in an attitude which
would have convulsed any ordinary man with
cramp. But there are few ordinary men in "K
(1)." There is never any difficulty in obtaining
volunteers for the Tunnelling Company.

So far as the amateur can penetrate its mys-

teries, mining, viewed under our present heading
— namely, Winter Sports — offers the following
advantages to its participants: —

(1) In winter it is much warmer below the earth
than upon its surface, and Thomas Atkins is the
most confirmed "frowster" in the world.

(2) Critics seldom descend into mines.

(3) There is extra pay.

The disadvantages are so obvious that they
need not be enumerated here.

In these trenches we have beei engaged upon a
very pretty game of subterranean chess for some
weeks past, and we are very much on our mettle.
We have some small leeway to make up. When
we took over these trenches, a German mine,
which had been maturing (apparently unheeded)
during the tenancy of our predecessors, was
exploded two days after our arrival, inflicting
heavy casualties upon "D" Company. Curiously
enough, the damage to the trench was comparatively slight; but the tremendous shock of the
explosion killed more than one man by concussion, and brought down the roofs of several dug-
outs upon their sleeping occupants. Altogether it
was a sad business, and the Battalion swore to be
avenged.

So they called upon Lieutenant Duff-Bertram
— usually called Bertie the Badger, in reference
to his rodent disposition — to make the first
move in the return match. So Bertie and his
troglodyte assistants sank a shaft in a retired spot
of their own selecting, and proceeded to burrow
forward towards the Boche lines.

After certain days Bertie presented himself,
covered in clay, before Colonel Kemp, and made a
report.

Colonel Kemp considered.

"You say you can hear the enemy working?"
he said.

"Yes, sir."

"Near?"

"Pretty near, sir."

"How near?"

"A few yards."

"What do you propose to do?"

Bertie the Badger — in private life he was a
consulting mining engineer with a beautiful office
in Victoria Street and a nice taste in spats —
scratched an earthy nose with a muddy forefinger.

"I think they are making a defensive gallery,
sir," he announced.

"Let us have your statement in the simplest
possible language, please," said Colonel Kemp.
"Some of my younger officers," he added rather
ingeniously, "are not very expert in these matters."

Bertie the Badger thereupon expounded the
situation with solemn relish. By a defensive gallery, it appeared that he meant a lateral tunnel
running parallel with the trench-line, in such a
manner as to intercept any tunnel pushed out by
the British miners.

"And what do you suggest doing to this Piccadilly Tube of theirs?" inquired the Colonel.

"I could dig forward and break into it, sir,"
suggested Bertie.

"That seems a move in the right direction," said the Colonel. "But won't the Boche try to prevent you?"

"Yes, sir."

"How?"

"He will wait until the head of my tunnel gets near enough, and then blow it in."

"That would be very tiresome of him. What other alternatives are open to you?"

"I could get as near as possible, sir," replied Bertie calmly, "and then blow up *his* gallery."

"That sounds better. Well, exercise your own discretion, and don't get blown up unless you particularly want to. And above all, be quite sure that while you are amusing yourself with the Piccadilly Tube, the wily Boche is n't burrowing past *you*, and under my parapet, by the Bakerloo! Good luck! Report any fresh development at once."

So Bertie the Badger returned once more to his native element and proceeded to exercise his discretion. This took the form of continuing his aggressive tunnel in the direction of the Boche defensive gallery. Next morning, encouraged by the absolute silence of the enemy's miners, he made a farther and final push, which actually landed him in the "Piccadilly Tube" itself.

"This is a rum go, Howie!" he observed in a low voice to his corporal. "A long, beautiful gallery, five by four, lined with wood, electrically lighted, with every modern convenience — and not a Boche in it!"

"Varra bad discipline, sir!" replied Corporal
Howie severely.

"Are you sure it is n't a trap?"

"It may be, sirr; but I doot the oversman is
awa' to his dinner, and the men are back in the
shaft, doing naething." Corporal Howie had been
an "oversman" himself, and knew something of
subterranean labour problems.

"Well, if you are right, the Boche must be
getting demoralised. It is not like him to present
us with openings like this. However, the first
thing to do is to distribute a few souvenirs along
the gallery. Pass the word back for the stuff.
Meanwhile I shall endeavour to test your theory
about the oversman's dinner-hour. I am going to
creep along and have a look at the Boche entrance to the Tube. It's down there, at the south
end, I think. I can see a break in the wood lining.
If you hear any shooting, you will know that the
dinner-hour is over!"

At the end of half an hour the Piccadilly Tube
was lined with sufficient explosive material — se-
curely rammed and tamped — to ensure the permanent closing of the line. Still no Boche had
been seen or heard.

"Now, Howie," said Bertie the Badger, finger-
ing the fuse, "what about it?"

"About what, sirr?" inquired Howie, who was
not quite *au fait* with current catch-phrases.

"Are we going to touch off all this stuff now,
and clear out, or are we going to wait and see?"

"I would like fine —" began the Corporal
wistfully.

"So would I," said Bertie. "Tell the men to get back and out; and you and I will hold on until the guests return from the banquet."

"Varra good, sirr."

For another half-hour the pair waited — Bertie the Badger like a dog in its kennel, with his head protruding into the hostile gallery, while his faithful henchman crouched close behind him. Deathly stillness reigned, relieved only by an occasional thud, as a shell or trench-mortar bomb exploded upon the ground above their heads.

"I'm going to have another look round the corner," said Bertie at last. "Hold on to the fuse."

He handed the end of the fuse to his subordinate, and having wormed his way out of the tunnel, proceeded cautiously on all-fours along the gallery. On his way he passed the electric light. He twisted off the bulb and crawled on in the dark.

Feeling his way by the east wall of the gallery, he came presently to the break in the woodwork. Very slowly, lying flat on his stomach now, he wriggled forward until his head came opposite the opening. A low passage ran away to his left, obviously leading back to the Boche trenches. Three yards from the entrance the passage bent sharply to the right, thus interrupting the line of sight.

"There's a light burning just round that bend," said Bertie the Badger to himself. "I wonder if it would be rash to go on and have a look at it!"

He was still straining at this gnat, when suddenly his elbow encountered a shovel which was leaning against the wall of the gallery. It tumbled down with a clatter almost stunning. Next moment a hand came round the bend of the tunnel and fired a revolver almost into the explorer's face.

Another shot rang out directly after.

The devoted Howie, hastening to the rescue, collided sharply with a solid body crawling towards him in the darkness.

"Curse you, Howie!" said the voice of Bertie the Badger, with refreshing earnestness. "Get back out of this! Where's your fuse?"

The pair scrambled back into their own tunnel, and the end of the fuse was soon recovered. Almost simultaneously three more revolver-shots rang out.

"I thought I had fixed that Boche," murmured Bertie in a disappointed voice. "I heard him grunt when my bullet hit him. Perhaps this is another one — or several. Keep back in the tunnel, Howie, confound you, and don't breathe up my sleeve! They are firing straight along the gallery now. I will return the compliment. Ouch!"

"What's the matter, sirr?" inquired the anxious voice of Howie, as his officer, who had tried to fire round the corner with his left hand, gave a sudden exclamation and rolled over upon his side.

"I must have been hit the first time," he explained. "Collar-bone, I think. I did n't know, till I rested my weight on my left elbow. . . . Howie, I am going to exercise my discretion again.

Somebody in this gallery is going to be blown up
presently, and if you and I don't get a move on,
p.d.q., it will be us! Give me the fuse-lighter, and
wait for me at the foot of the shaft. Quick!"

Very reluctantly the Corporal obeyed. However, he was in due course joined at the foot of the
shaft by Bertie the Badger, groaning profanely;
and the pair made their way to the upper regions
with all possible speed. After a short interval, a
sudden rumbling, followed by a heavy explosion,
announced that the fuse had done its work, and
that the Piccadilly Tube, the fruit of many toil-
some weeks of Boche calculation and labour, had
been permanently closed to traffic of all descrip-
tions.

Bertie the Badger received a Military Cross,
and his abettor the D.C.M.

v

But the newest and most fashionable form of
winter sport this season is The Flying Matinée.

This entertainment takes place during the
small hours of the morning, and is strictly limited
to a duration of ten minutes — quite long enough
for most matinées, too. The actors are furnished
by a unit of "K (1)" and the rôle of audience is
assigned to the inhabitants of the Boche trenches
immediately opposite. These matinées have
proved an enormous success, but require most
careful rehearsal.

It is two A.M., and comparative peace reigns up
and down the line. The rain of star-shells, always
prodigal in the early evening, has died down to a

mere drizzle. Working and fatigue parties, which have been busy since darkness set in at five o'clock, — rebuilding parapets, repairing wire, carrying up rations, and patrolling debatable areas, — have ceased their labours, and are sleeping heavily until the coming of the wintry dawn shall rouse them, grimy and shivering, to another day's unpleasantness.

Private Hans Dumpkopf, on sentry duty in the Boche firing-trench, gazes mechanically over the parapet; but the night is so dark and the wind so high that it is difficult to see and quite impossible to hear anything. He shelters himself beside a traverse, and waits patiently for his relief. It begins to rain, and Hans, after cautiously reconnoitring the other side of the traverse, to guard against prowling sergeants, sidles a few yards to his right beneath the friendly cover of an improvised roof of corrugated iron sheeting, laid across the trench from parapet to parados. It is quite dry here, and comparatively warm. Hans closes his eyes for a moment, and heaves a gentle sigh.

Next moment there comes a rush of feet in the darkness, followed by a metallic clang, as of hob-nailed boots on metal. Hans, lying prostrate and half-stunned beneath the galvanised iron sheeting, which, dislodged from its former position by the impact of a heavy body descending from above, now forms part of the flooring of the trench, is suddenly aware that this same trench is full of men — rough, uncultured men, clad in short petticoats and the skins of wild animals, and armed with knobkerries. The Flying Matinée has begun, and Hans Dumpkopf has got in by the early door.

Each of the performers — there are fifty of them all told — has his part to play, and plays it with commendable aplomb. One, having disarmed an unresisting prisoner, assists him over the parapet and escorts him affectionately to his new home. Another clubs a recalcitrant foeman over the head with a knobkerry, and having thus reduced him to a more amenable frame of mind, hoists him over the parapet and drags him after his "kamarad."

Other parties are told off to deal with the dugouts. As a rule, the occupants of these are too dazed to make any resistance, — to be quite frank, the individual Boche in these days seems rather to welcome captivity than otherwise, — and presently more of the "bag" are on their way to the British lines.

But by this time the performance is drawing to a close. The alarm has been communicated to the adjacent sections of the trench, and preparations for the ejection of the intruders are being hurried forward. That is to say, German bombers are collecting upon either flank, with the intention of bombing "inwards" until the impudent foe has been destroyed or evicted. As we are not here to precipitate a general action, but merely to round up a few prisoners and do as much damage as possible in ten minutes, we hasten to the finale. As in most finales, one's actions now become less restrained — but, from a brutal point of view, more

effective. A couple of hand-grenades are thrown
into any dug-out which has not yet surrendered.
(The Canadians, who make quite a speciality of
flying matinées, are accustomed, we understand,
as an artistic variant to this practice, to fasten an
electric torch along the barrel of a rifle, and so
illuminate their lurking targets while they shoot.)
A sharp order passes along the line; every one
scrambles out of the trench; and the troupe makes
its way back, before the enemy in the adjacent
trenches have really wakened up, to the place
from which it came. The matinée, so far as the
actors are concerned, is over.

Not so the audience. The avenging host is
just getting busy. The bombing-parties are now
marshalled and proceed with awful solemnity
and Teutonic thoroughness to clear the violated
trench. The procedure of a bombing-party is
stereotyped. They begin by lobbing hand-grenades over the first traverse into the first bay.
After the ensuing explosion, they trot round the
traverse in single file and occupy the bay. This
manœuvre is then repeated until the entire trench
is cleared. The whole operation requires good
discipline, considerable courage, and carefully
timed co-operation with the other bombing-
party. In all these attributes the Boche excels.
But one thing is essential to the complete success
of his efforts, and that is the presence of the enemy. When, after methodically desolating each
bay in turn (and incidentally killing their own
wounded in the process), the two parties meet
midway — practically on top of the unfortunate

Hans Dumpkopf, who is still giving an imitation of a tortoise in a corrugated shell — it is discovered that the beautifully executed counter-attack has achieved nothing but the recapture of an entirely empty trench. The birds have flown, taking their prey with them. Hans is the sole survivor, and after hearing what his officer has to say to him upon the subject, bitterly regrets the fact.

Meanwhile, in the British trenches a few yards away, the box-office returns are being made up. These take the form, firstly, of some twenty-five prisoners, including one indignant officer — he had been pulled from his dug-out half asleep and frog-marched across the British lines by two private soldiers well qualified to appreciate the richness of his language — together with various souvenirs in the way of arms and accoutrements; and secondly, of the knowledge that at least as many more of the enemy had been left permanently incapacitated for further warfare in the dug-outs. A grim and grisly drama when you come to criticise it in cold blood, but not without a certain humour of its own — and most educative for Brother Boche!

But he is a slow pupil. He regards the profession of arms and the pursuit of war with such intense and solemn reverence that he *cannot* conceive how any one calling himself a soldier can be so criminally frivolous as to write a farce round the subject — much less present the farce at a Flying Matinée. That possibly explains why the following stately paragraph appeared a few days later in the periodical communiqué which keeps the German nation in touch with its Army's latest exploits: —

During the night of Jan. 4th-5th attempts were made by strong detachments of the enemy to penetrate our line near Sloozleschump, S.E. of Ypres. The attack failed utterly.

"And they don't even realise that it was only a leg-pull!" commented the Company Commander who had stage-managed the affair. "These people simply don't deserve to have entertainments arranged for them at all. Well, we must pull the limb again, that's all!"

And it was so.

IV

I

"I WONDER if they really mean business this time," surmised that youthful Company Commander, Temporary Captain Bobby Little, to Major Wagstaffe.

"It sounds like it," said Wagstaffe, as another salvo of "whizz-bangs" broke like inflammatory surf upon the front-line trenches. "Intermittent *strafes* we are used to, but this all-day performance seems to indicate that the Boche is really getting down to it for once. The whole proceeding reminds me of nothing so much as our own 'artillery preparation' before the big push at Loos."

"Then you think the Boches are going to make a push of their own?"

"I do; and I hope it will be a good fat one. When it comes, I fancy we shall be able to put up something rather pretty in the way of a defence. The Salient is stiff with guns — I don't think the Boche quite realises *how* stiff! And we owe the swine something!" he added through his teeth.

There was a pause in the conversation. You cannot hold the Salient for three months without paying for the distinction; and the regiment had paid its full share. Not so much in numbers, perhaps, as in quality. Stray bullets, whistling up and down the trenches, coming even obliquely

from the rear, had exacted most grievous toll.
Shells and trench-mortar bombs, taking us in
flank, had extinguished many valuable lives. At
this time nothing but the best seemed to satisfy
the Fates. One day it would be a trusted colour-
sergeant, on another a couple of particularly
promising young corporals. Only last week the
Adjutant — athlete, scholar, born soldier, and
very lovable schoolboy, all most perfectly blended
— had fallen mortally wounded, on his morning
round of the fire-trenches, by a bullet which came
from nowhere. He was the subject of Wagstaffe's reference.

"Is it not possible," suggested Mr. Waddell,
who habitually considered all questions from
every possible point of view, "that this bombardment has been specially initiated by the German
authorities, in order to impress upon their own
troops a warning that there must be no Christmas
truce this year?"

"If that is the Kaiser's Christmas greeting to
his loving followers," observed Wagstaffe drily,
"I think he might safely have left it to us to
deliver it!"

"They say," interposed Bobby Little, "that
the Kaiser is here himself."

"How do you know?"

"It was rumoured in 'Comic Cuts.'" ("Comic
Cuts" is the stately Summary of War Intelligence issued daily from Olympus.)

"If that is true," said Wagstaffe, "they probably will attack. All this fuss and bobbery suggest
something of the kind. They remind me of the

commotion which used to precede Arthur Roberts's entrance in the old days of Gaiety burlesque. Before your time, I fancy, Bobby?"

"Yes," said Bobby modestly. "I first found touch with the Gaiety over 'Our Miss Gibbs.' And I was quite a kid even then," he added, with characteristic honesty. "But what about Arthur Roberts?"

"Some forty or fifty years ago," explained Wagstaffe, "when I was in the habit of frequenting places of amusement, Arthur Roberts was leading man at the establishment to which I have referred. He usually came on about half-past eight, just as the show was beginning to lose its first wind. His entrance was a most tremendous affair. First of all the entire chorus blew in from the wings — about sixty of them in ten seconds — saying "Hurrah, hurrah, girls!" or something rather subtle of that kind; after which minor characters rushed on from opposite sides and told one another that Arthur Roberts was coming. Then the band played, and everybody began to tell the audience about it in song. When everything was in full blast, the great man would appear — stepping out of a bathing-machine, or falling out of a hansom-cab, or sliding down a chute on a toboggan. He was assisted to his feet by the chorus, and then proceeded to ginger the show up. Well, that's how this present entertainment impresses me. All this noise and obstreperousness are leading up to one thing — Kaiser Bill's entrance. Preliminary bombardment — that's the chorus getting to work! Minor characters — the trench-mortars — spread the glad news! Band *and* chorus — that's the grand attack working up to boiling-point! Finally, preceded by clouds of gas, the Arch-Comedian in person, supported by spectacled coryphées in brass hats! How's that for a Christmas pantomime?"

"Rotten!" said Bobby, as a shell sang over the parapet and burst in the wood behind.

II

Kaiser or no Kaiser, Major Wagstaffe's extravagant analogy held good. As Christmas drew nearer, the band played louder and faster; the chorus swelled higher and shriller; and it became finally apparent that something (or somebody) of portentous importance was directing the storm.

Between six and seven next morning, the Battalion, which had stood to arms all night, lifted up its heavy head and sniffed the misty dawn-wind — an east wind — dubiously. Next moment gongs were clanging up and down the trench, and men were tearing open the satchels which contained their anti-gas helmets.

Major Wagstaffe, who had been sent up from Battalion Headquarters to take general charge of affairs in the firing-trench, buttoned the bottom edge of his helmet well inside his collar and clambered up on the firing-step to take stock of the position. He crouched low, for a terrific bombardment was in progress, and shells were almost grazing the parapet.

Presently he was joined by a slim young officer

similarly disguised. It was the Commander of
"A" Company. Wagstaffe placed his head close
to Bobby's left ear, and shouted through the
cloth —

"We shan't feel this gas much. They're letting
it off higher up the line. Look!"

Bobby, laboriously inhaling the tainted air inside his helmet, — being preserved from a gas
attack is only one degree less unpleasant than
being gassed, — turned his goggles northward.

In the dim light of the breaking day he could
discern a greenish-yellow cloud rolling across from
the Boche trenches on his left.

"Will they attack?" he bellowed.

Wagstaffe nodded his head, and then cautiously
unbuttoned his collar and rolled up the front of
his helmet. Then, after delicately sampling the
atmosphere by a cautious sniff, he removed his
helmet altogether. Bobby followed his example.
The air was not by any means so pure as might
have been desired, but it was infinitely preferable
to that inside a gas-helmet.

"Nothing to signify," pronounced Wagstaffe.
"We're only getting the edge of it. Sergeant, pass
down that men may roll up their helmets, but
must keep them on their heads. Now, Bobby,
things are getting interesting. Will they attack,
or will they not?"

"What do you think?" asked Bobby.

"They are certainly going to attack farther
north. The Boche does not waste gas as a rule —
not this sort of gas! And I think he'll attack here
too. The only reason why he has not switched on

our anæsthetic is that the wind is n't quite right
for this bit of the line. I think it is going to be a
general push. Bobby, have a look through this
sniper's loophole. Can you see any bayonets
twinkling in the Boche trenches?"

Bobby applied an eye to the loophole.

"Yes," he said, "I can see them. Those
trenches must be packed with men."

"Absolutely stiff with them," agreed Wagstaffe, getting out his revolver. "We shall be in
for it presently. Are your fellows all ready,
Bobby?"

The youthful Captain ran his eye along the
trench, where his Company, with magazines
loaded and bayonets fixed, were grimly awaiting
the onset. There had been an onset similar to this,
with the same green, nauseous accompaniment, in
precisely the same spot eight months before,
which had broken the line and penetrated for four
miles. There it had been stayed by a forlorn hope
of cooks, brakesmen, and officers' servants, and
disaster had been most gloriously retrieved.
What was going to happen this time? One thing
was certain: the day of stink-pots was over.

"When do you think they'll attack?" shouted
Bobby to Wagstaffe, battling against the noise of
bursting shells.

"Quite soon — in a minute or two. Their guns
will stop directly — to lift their sights and set up
a barrage behind us. Then, perhaps the Boche
will step over his parapet. Perhaps not!"

The last sentence rang out with uncanny dis-
tinctness, for the German guns with one accord

had ceased firing. For a full two minutes there was absolute silence, while the bayonets in the opposite trenches twinkled with tenfold intent.

Then, from every point in the great Salient of Ypres, the British guns replied.

Possibly the Imperial General Staff at Berlin had been misinformed as to the exact strength of the British Artillery. Possibly they had been informed by their Intelligence Department that Trades Unionism, had ensured that a thoroughly inadequate supply of shells was to hand in the Salient. Or possibly they had merely decided, after the playful habit of General Staffs, to let the infantry in the trenches take their chance of any retaliation that might be forthcoming.

Whatever these great men were expecting, it is highly improbable that they expected that which arrived. Suddenly the British batteries spoke out, and they all spoke together. In the space of four minutes they deposited *thirty thousand* high-explosive shells in the Boche front-line trenches — yea, distributed the same accurately and evenly along all that crowded arc. Then they paused, as suddenly as they began, while British riflemen and machine-gunners bent to their work.

But few received the order to fire. Here and there a wave of men broke over the German parapet and rolled towards the British lines — only to be rolled back crumpled up by machine-guns. Never once was the goal reached. The great Christmas attack was over. After months of weary waiting and foolish recrimination, that exasperating race of bad starters but great stay-ers, the British people, had delivered "the goods," and made it possible for their soldiers to speak with the enemy in the gate upon equal — nay, superior, terms.

"Is that all?" asked Bobby Little, peering out over the parapet, a little awe-struck, at the devastation over the way.

"That is all," said Wagstaffe, "or I'm a Boche! There will be much noise and some irregular scrapping for days, but the tin lid has been placed upon the grand attack. The great Christmas Victory is off!"

Then he added, thoughtfully, referring apparently to the star performer: —

"We *have* been and spoiled his entrance for him, have n't we?"

V

I

THERE is a certain type of English country-house
female who is said to "live in her boxes." That is
to say, she appears to possess no home of her own,
but flits from one indulgent roof-tree to another;
and owing to the fact that she is invariably put
into a bedroom whose wardrobe is full of her hostess's superannuated ball-frocks and winter furs,
never knows what it is to have all her "things"
unpacked at once.

Well, we out here cannot be said to live in our
boxes, for we do not possess any; but we do most
undoubtedly live in our haversacks and packs.
And this brings us to the matter in hand —
namely, so-called "Rest-Billets." The whole of
the hinterland of this great trench-line is full of
tired men, seeking for a place to lie down in, and
living in their boxes when they find one.

At present we are indulging in such a period of
repose; and we venture to think that on the whole
we have earned it. Our last rest was in high summer, when we lay about under an August sun in
the district round Béthune, and called down
curses upon all flying and creeping insects. Since
then we have undergone certain so-called "operations" in the neighbourhood of Loos, and have
put in three months in the Salient of Ypres. As

that devout adherent of the Roman faith, Private
Reilly, of "B" Company, put it to his spiritual
adviser —

"I doot we'll get excused a good slice of Pur-
gatory for this, father!"

We came out of the Salient just before Christmas, in the midst of the mutual unpleasantness
arising out of the grand attack upon the British
line which was to have done so much to restore
the waning confidence of the Hun. It was meant
to be a big affair — a most majestic victory, in
fact; but our new gas-helmets nullified the gas,
and our new shells paralysed the attack; so the
Third Battle of Ypres was not yet. Still, as I say,
there was considerable unpleasantness all round;
and we were escorted upon our homeward way,
from Sanctuary Wood to Zillebeke, and from
Zillebeke to Dickebusche, by a swarm of angry
and disappointed shells.

Next day we found ourselves many miles behind the firing-line, once more in France, with a
whole month's holiday in prospect, comfortably
conscious that one could walk round a corner or
look over a wall without preliminary reconnaissance or subsequent extirpation.

As for the holiday itself, unreasonable persons
are not lacking to point out that it is of the bus-
man's variety. It is true that we are no longer
face to face with the foe, but we — or rather, the
authorities — make believe that we are. We wage
mimic warfare in full marching order; we fire rifles
and machine-guns upon improvised ranges; we
perform hazardous feats with bombs and a

dummy trench. More galling still, we are back in
the region of squad-drill, physical exercises, and
handling of arms — horrors of our childhood
which we thought had been left safely interned at
Aldershot.

But the authorities are wise. The regiment is
stiff and out of condition: it is suffering from
moral and intellectual "trench-feet." Heavy
drafts have introduced a large and untempered
element into our composition. Many of the
subalterns are obviously "new-jined" — as the
shrewd old lady of Ayr once observed of the rubi-
cund gentleman at the temperance meeting.
Their men hardly know them or one another
by sight. The regiment must be moulded anew,
and its lustre restored by the beneficent process
vulgarly known as "spit and polish." So every
morning we apply ourselves with thoroughness, if
not enthusiasm, to tasks which remind us of last
winter's training upon the Hampshire chalk.

But the afternoon and evening are a different
story altogether. If we were busy in the morning,
we are busier still for the rest of the day. There is
football galore, for we have to get through a complete series of Divisional cup-ties in four weeks.
There is also a Brigade boxing-tournament. (No,
that was not where Private Tosh got his black
eye: that is a souvenir of New Year's Eve.) There
are entertainments of various kinds in the recre-
ation-tent. This whistling platoon, with towels
round their necks, are on their way to the nearest
convent, or asylum, or École des Jeunes Filles —
have no fear; these establishments are unten-

anted! — for a bath. There, in addition to the
pleasures of ablution, they will receive a partial
change of raiment.

Other signs of regeneration are visible. That
mysterious-looking vehicle, rather resembling one
of the early locomotives exhibited in the South
Kensington Museum, standing in the mud outside
a farm-billet, its superheated interior stuffed with
"C" Company's blankets, is performing an un-
mentionable but beneficent work.

Buttons are resuming their polish; the pattern
of our kilts is emerging from its superficial crust;
and Church Parade is once more becoming quite a
show affair.

Away to the east the guns still thunder, and at
night the star-shells float tremblingly up over the
distant horizon. But not for us. Not yet, that is.
In a few weeks' time we shall be back in another
part of the line. Till then — Company drill and
Cup-Ties! *Carpe diem!*

II

It all seemed very strange and unreal to Second-
Lieutenant Angus M'Lachlan, as he alighted from
the train at railhead, and supervised the efforts of
his solitary N.C.O. to arrange the members of his
draft in a straight line. There were some thirty of
them in all. Some were old hands — men from
the First and Second Battalions, who had been
home wounded, and had now been sent out to
leaven "K (1)." Others were Special Reservists
from the Third Battalion. These had been at the
Dépôt for a long time, and some of them stood

badly in need of a little active service. Others, again, were new hands altogether — the product of "K to the $n^{th.}$" Among these Angus M'Lachlan numbered himself, and he made no attempt to conceal the fact. The novelty of the sights around him was almost too much for his *insouciant* dignity as a commissioned officer.

Angus M'Lachlan was a son of the Manse, and incidentally a child of Nature. The Manse was a Highland Manse; and until a few months ago Angus had never, save for a rare visit to distant Edinburgh, penetrated beyond the small town which lay four miles from his native glen, and of whose local Academy he had been "dux." When the War broke out he had been upon the point of proceeding to Edinburgh University, where he had already laid siege to a bursary, and captured the same; but all these plans, together with the plans of countless more distinguished persons, had been swept to the winds by the invasion of Belgium. On that date Angus summoned up his entire stock of physical and moral courage and informed his reverend parent of his intention to enlist for a soldier. Permission was granted with quite stunning readiness. Neil M'Lachlan believed in straight hitting both in theology and war, and was by no means displeased at the martial aspirations of his only son. If he quitted himself like a man in the forefront of battle, the boy could safely look forward to being cock of his own Kirk-Session in the years that came afterwards. One reservation the old man made. His son, as a Highland gentleman, would lead men to battle, and not merely accompany them. So the impatient Angus was bidden to apply for a Commission — his attention during the period of waiting being directed by his parent to the study of the campaigns of Joshua, and the methods employed by that singular but successful strategist in dealing with the Philistine.

Angus had a long while to wait, for all the youth of England — and Scotland too — was on fire, and others nearer the fountain of honour had to be served first. But his turn came at last; and we now behold him, as typical a product of "K to the nth" as Bobby Little had been of "K (1)," standing at last upon the soil of France, and inquiring in a soft Highland voice for the Headquarters of our own particular Battalion.

He had half expected, half hoped, to alight from the train amidst a shower of shells, as he knew the Old Regiment had done many months before, just after the War broke out. But all he saw upon his arrival was an untidy goods yard, littered with military stores, and peopled by British privates in the *déshabille* affected by the British Army when engaged in menial tasks.

Being quite ignorant of the whereabouts of his regiment — when last heard of they had been in trenches near Ypres — and failing to recollect the existence of that autocratic but indispensable *genius loci*, the R.T.O., Angus took uneasy stock of his surroundings and wondered what to do next.

Suddenly a friendly voice at his elbow remarked —

"There's a queer lot o' bodies hereaboot, sirr."

Angus turned, to find that he was being addressed by a short, stout private of the draft, in a kilt much too big for him.

"Indeed, that is so," he replied politely. "What is your name?"

"Peter Bogle, sirr. I am frae oot of Kirkintilloch." Evidently gratified by the success of his conversational opening, the little man continued —

"I would like fine for tae get a contrack oot here after the War. This country is in a terrible state o' disrepair." Then he added confidentially —

"I'm a hoose-painter tae a trade."

"I should not like to be that myself," replied Angus, whose early training as a minister's son was always causing him to forget the social gulf which is fixed between officers and the rank-and-file. "Climbing ladders makes me dizzy."

"Och, it's naething! A body gets used tae it," Mr. Bogle assured him.

Angus was about to proceed further with the discussion, when the cold and disapproving voice of the Draft-Sergeant announced in his ear —

"An officer wishes to speak to you, sir."

Second-Lieutenant M'Lachlan, suddenly awake to the enormity of his conduct, turned guiltily to greet the officer, while the Sergeant abruptly hunted the genial Private Bogle back into the ranks.

Angus found himself confronted by an immaculate young gentleman wearing two stars. Angus, who only wore one, saluted hurriedly.

"Morning," observed the stranger. "You in charge of this draft?"

"Yes, sir," said Angus respectfully.

"Right-o! You are to march them to 'A' Company billets. I'll show you the way. My name's Cockerell. Your train is late. What time did you leave the Base?"

"Indeed," replied Angus meekly, "I am not quite sure. We had barely landed when they told me the train would start at seventeen-forty. What time would that be — sir?"

"About a quarter to ten: more likely about midnight! Well, get your bunch on to the road, and — Hallo, what's the matter? Let go!"

The new officer was gripping him excitedly by the arm, and as the new officer stood six-foot-four and was brawny in proportion, Master Cockerell's appeal was uttered in a tone of unusual sincerity.

"Look!" cried Angus excitedly. "The dogs, the dogs!"

A small cart was passing swiftly by, towed by two sturdy hounds of unknown degree. They were pulling with the feverish enthusiasm which distinguishes the Dog in the service of Man, and were being urged to further efforts by a small hatless girl carrying the inevitable large umbrella.

"All right!" explained Cockerell curtly. "Custom of the country, and all that."

The impulsive Angus apologised; and the draft, having been safely manœuvred on to the road, formed fours and set out upon its march.

"Are the Battalion in the trenches at present, sir?" inquired Angus.

"No. Rest-billets two miles from here. About time, too! You'll get lots of work to do, though."

"I shall welcome that," said Angus simply. "In the dépôt at home we were terribly idle. There is a windmill!"

"Yes; one sees them occasionally out here," replied Cockerell drily.

"Everything is so strange!" confessed the open-hearted Angus. "Those dogs we saw just now — the people with their sabots — the country carts, like wheelbarrows with three wheels — the little shrines at the cross-roads — the very children talking French so glibly —"

"Wonderful how they pick it up!" agreed Cockerell. But the sarcasm was lost on his companion, whose attention was now riveted upon an approaching body of infantry, about fifty strong.

"What troops are those, please?"

Cockerell knitted his brows sardonically.

"It's rather hard to tell at this distance," he said; "but I rather think they are the Grenadier Guards."

Two minutes later the procession had been met and passed. It consisted entirely of elderly gentlemen in ill-fitting khaki, clumping along upon their flat feet and smoking clay pipes. They carried shovels on their shoulders, and made not the slightest response when called upon by the soldierly old corporal who led them to give Mr. Cockerell "eyes left!" On the contrary, engaged as they were in heated controversy or amiable conversation with one another, they cut him dead.

Angus M'Lachlan said nothing for quite five minutes. Then —

"I suppose," he said almost timidly, "that those were members of a *Reserve* Regiment of the Guards?"

Cockerell, who had never outgrown certain characteristics which most of us shed upon emerging from the Lower Fourth, laughed long and loud.

"That crowd? They belong to one of the Labour Battalions. They make roads, and dig support trenches, and sling mud about generally. Wonderful old sportsmen! Pleased as Punch when a shell falls within half a mile of them. Something to write home about. What? I say, I pulled your leg that time! Here we are at Headquarters. Come and report to the C.O. Grenadier Guards! My aunt!"

Angus, although his Celtic enthusiasm sometimes led him into traps, was no fool. He soon settled down in his new surroundings, and found favour with Colonel Kemp, which was no light achievement.

"You won't find that the War, in its present stage, calls for any display of genius," the Colonel explained to Angus at their first interview. "I don't expect my officers to exhibit any quality but the avoidance of *sloppiness*. If I detail you to be at a certain spot, at a certain hour, with a certain number of men — a ration-party, or a working-party, or a burial-party, or anything you like, — all I ask is that you will be *there*, at the appointed hour, with the whole of your following. That may not sound a very difficult feat, but experience has taught me that if a man can achieve it, and can be *relied* upon to achieve it, say, nine times out of ten—well, he is a pearl of price; and there is not a C.O. in the British Army who would n't scramble to get him! That's all, M'Lachlan. Good morning!"

By punctilious attention to this sound advice Angus soon began to build up a reputation. He treated war-worn veterans like Bobby Little with immense respect, and this, too, was counted to him for righteousness. He exercised his platoon with appalling vigour. Upon Company route-marches he had to be embedded in some safe place in the middle of the column; in fact, his enormous stride and pedestrian enthusiasm would have reduced his followers to pulp. At Mess he was mute: like a wise man, he was feeling for his feet.

But being, like Moses, slow of tongue, he provided himself with an Aaron. Quite inadvertently, be it said. Bidden to obtain a servant for his personal needs, he selected the only man in the Battalion whose name he knew — Private Bogle, the *ci-devant* painter of houses. That friendly creature obeyed the call with alacrity. If his house-painting was no better than his valeting, then his prospects of a "contrack" after the War were poor indeed; but as a Mess waiter he was a joy for ever. Despite the blood-curdling whispers of the Mess Corporal, his natural urbanity of disposition could not be stemmed. Of the comfort of others he was solicitous to the point of oppressiveness. A Mess waiter's idea of efficiency as a rule is to stand woodenly at attention in an obscure corner of the room. When called upon, he starts forward with a jerk, and usually trips over something — probably his own feet. Not so Private Bogle.

"Wull you try another cup o' tea, Major?" he would suggest at breakfast to Major Wagstaffe, leaning affectionately over the back of his chair.

"No, thank you, Bogle," Major Wagstaffe would reply gravely.

"Weel, it's cauld onyway," Bogle would rejoin, anxious to endorse his superior's decision.

Or — in the same spirit —

"Wull I luft the soup now, sir?"

"*No!*"

"Varra weel: I'll jist let it bide the way it is."

Lastly, Angus M'Lachlan proved himself a useful acquisition — especially in rest-billets — as an athlete. He arrived just in time to take part — no mean part, either — in a Rugby Football match played between the officers of two Brigades. Thanks very largely to his masterly leading of the forwards, our Brigade were preserved from defeat at the hands of their opponents, who on paper had appeared to be irresistible.

Rugby Football "oot here" is a rarity, though Association, being essentially the game of the rank-and-file, flourishes in every green field. But an Inverleith or Queen's Club crowd would have recognised more than one old friend among the

thirty who took the field that day. There were
those participating whose last game had been one
of the spring "Internationals" in 1914, and who
had been engaged in a prolonged and strenuous
version of an even greater International ever
since August of that fateful year. Every public
school in Scotland was represented —sometimes
three or four times over — and there were numerous doughty contributions from establishments
south of the Tweed.

The lookers-on were in different case. They
were to a man devoted — nay, frenzied — ad-
herents of the rival code. In less spacious days
they had surged in their thousands every Saturday afternoon to Ibrox, or Tynecastle, or Park-
head, there to yell themselves into convulsions —
now exhorting a friend to hit some one a kick on
the nose, now recommending the foe to play the
game, now hoarsely consigning the referee to per-
dition. To these, Rugby Football — the greatest
of all manly games — was a mere name. Their
attitude when the officers appeared upon the field
was one of indulgent superiority — the sort of
superiority that a brawny pitman exhibits when
his Platoon Commander steps down into a trench
to lend a hand with the digging.

But in five minutes their mouths were agape
with scandalised astonishment; in ten, the heavens were rent with their protesting cries. Accustomed to see football played with the feet, and to
demand with one voice the instant execution of
any player (on the other side) who laid so much as
a finger upon the ball or the man who was playing

it, the exhibition of savage and promiscuous bru-
tality to which their superior officers now treated
them shocked the assembled spectators to the
roots of their sensitive souls. Howls of virtuous
indignation burst forth upon all sides.

When the three-quarter-backs brought off a
brilliant passing run, there were stern cries of
"Haands, there, referee!" When Bobby Little
stopped an ugly rush by hurling himself on the
ball, the supporters of the other Brigade greeted
his heroic devotion with yells of execration. When
Angus M'Lachlan saved a certain try by tackling
a speedy wing three-quarter low and bringing him
down with a crash, a hundred voices demanded
his removal from the field. And, when Mr. Waddell, playing a stuffy but useful game at half,
gained fifty yards for his side by a series of
judicious little kicks into touch, the spectators
groaned aloud, and remarked caustically —

"This maun be a Cup-Tie, boys! They are
playin' for a draw, for tae get a second gate!"

Altogether a thoroughly enjoyable afternoon,
both for players and spectators. And so home to
tea, domesticity, and social intercourse. In this
connection it may be noted that our relations with
the inhabitants are of the friendliest. On the
stroke of six — oh yes, we have our licensing re-
strictions out here too! — half a dozen kilted war-
riors stroll into the farm-kitchen, and mumble
affably to Madame —

"Bone sworr! Beer?"

France boasts one enormous advantage over
Scotland. At home, you have at least to walk to

the corner of the street to obtain a drink: "oot
here" you can purchase beer in practically every
house in a village. The French licensing laws are
a thing of mystery, but the system appears
roughly to be this. Either you possess a license,
or you do not. If you do, you may sell beer, and
nothing else. If you do not, you may — or at any
rate do — sell anything you like, including beer.

However, we have left our friends thirsty.

Their wants are supplied with cheerful alacrity,
and, having been accommodated with seats round
the stove, they converse with the family. Heaven
only knows what they talk about, but talk they
do — in the throaty unintelligible Doric of the
Clydeside, with an occasional Gallicism, like,
"Allyman no bon!" or "Compree?" thrown in as
a sop to foreign idiosyncracies. Madame and
family respond, chattering French (or Flemish) at
enormous speed. The amazing part of it all is that
neither side appears to experience the slightest
difficulty in understanding the other. One day
Mr. Waddell, in the course of a friendly chat with
his hostess of the moment — she was unable to
speak a word of English — received her warm
congratulations upon his contemplated union
with a certain fair one of St. Andrew (to whom
reference has previously been made in these
pages). Mr. Waddell, a very fair linguist, replied
in suitable but embarrassed terms, and asked for
the source of the good lady's information.

"Mais votre ordonnance, m'sieur!" was the
reply.

Tackled upon the subject, the "ordonnance" in

question, Waddell's servant — a shock-headed
youth from Dundee — admitted having communicated the information; and added —

"She's a decent body, sirr, the lady o' the
hoose. She lost her husband, she was tellin' me,
three years ago. She has twa sons in the Airmy.
Her auld Auntie is up at the top o' the hoose —
lyin' badly, and no expectin' tae rise."

And yet some people study Esperanto!

We also make ourselves useful. "K (1)" con-
tains members of every craft. If the pig-sty door
is broken, a carpenter is forthcoming to mend it.
Somebody's elbow goes through a pane of glass in
the farm-kitchen: straightway a glazier material-
ises from the nearest platoon, and puts in another.
The ancestral eight-day clock of the household
develops internal complications; and is forthwith
dismembered and reassembled, "with punctual-
ity, civility, and despatch," by a gentleman who
until a few short months ago had done nothing
else for fifteen years.

And it was in this connection that Corporal
Mucklewame stumbled on to a rare and congenial
job, and incidentally made the one joke of his life.

One afternoon a cow, the property of Madame
la fermière, developed symptoms of some serious
disorder. A period of dolorous bellowing was followed by an outburst of homicidal mania, during
which "A" Company prudently barricaded itself
into the barn, the sufferer having taken entire
possession of the farmyard. Next, and finally —
so rapidly did the malady run its course — a state
of coma intervened; and finally the cow, collaps-

ing upon the doorstep of the Officers' Mess, breathed her last before any one could be found to point out to her the liberty she was taking.

It was decided to hold a *post-mortem* — firstly, to ascertain the cause of death; secondly, because it is easier to remove a dead cow after dissection than before. Madame therefore announced her intention of sending for the butcher, and was upon the point of doing so when Corporal Mucklewame, in whose heart, at the spectacle of the stark and lifeless corpse, ancient and romantic memories were stirring — it may be remembered that before answering to the call of "K (1)" Mucklewame had followed the calling of butcher's assistant at Wishaw — volunteered for the job. His services were cordially accepted by thrifty Madame; and the Corporal, surrounded by a silent and admiring crowd, set to work.

The officers, leaving the Junior Subaltern in charge, went with one accord for a long country walk.

Half an hour later Mucklewame arrived at the seat of the deceased animal's trouble — the seat of most of the troubles of mankind — its stomach. After a brief investigation, he produced therefrom a small bag of nails, recently missed from the vicinity of a cook-house in course of construction in the corner of the yard.

Abandoning the rôle of surgical expert for that of coroner, Mucklewame held the trophy aloft, and delivered his verdict —

"There, boys! That's what comes of eating your iron ration without authority!"

III

Here is an average billet, and its personnel.

The central feature of our residence is the refuse-pit, which fills practically the whole of the rectangular farmyard, and resembles (in size and shape *only*) an open-air swimming bath. Its abundant contents are apparently the sole asset of the household; for if you proceed, in the interests of health, to spread a decent mantle of honest earth thereover, you do so to the accompaniment of a harmonised chorus of lamentation, very creditably rendered by the entire family, who are grouped *en masse* about the spot where the high diving-board ought to be.

Round this perverted place of ablution runs a stone ledge, some four feet wide, and round that again run the farm buildings — the house at the top end, a great barn down one side, and the cow-house, together with certain darksome piggeries and fowl-houses, down the other. These latter residences are occupied only at night, their tenants preferring to spend the golden hours of day in profitable occupation upon the happy hunting ground in the middle.

Within the precincts of this already over-crowded establishment are lodged some two hundred British soldiers and their officers. The men sleep in the barn, their meals being prepared for them upon the Company cooker, which stands in the muddy road outside, and resembles the humble vehicle employed by Urban District Councils for the preparation of tar for road-

mending purposes. The officers occupy any room
which may be available within the farmhouse itself. The Company Commander has the best bedroom — a low-roofed, stone-floored apartment,
with a very small window and a very large bed.
The subalterns sleep where they can — usually in
the *grenier*, a loft under the tiles, devoted to the
storage of onions and the drying, during the winter months, of the family washing, which is sus-
pended from innumerable strings stretched from
wall to wall.

For a Mess, there is usually a spare apartment
of some kind. If not, you put your pride in your
pocket and take your meals at the kitchen table,
at such hours as the family are not sitting humped
round the same with their hats on, partaking of
soup or coffee. (This appears to be their sole sus-
tenance.) A farm-kitchen in northern France is a
scrupulously clean place — the whole family gets
up at half-past four in the morning and sees to the
matter — and despite the frugality of her own
home *menu*, the *fermière* can produce you a perfect
omelette at any hour of the day or night.

This brings us to the kitchen-stove, which is a
marvel. No massive and extravagant English
ranges here! There is only one kind: we call it the
Coffin and Flower-pot. The coffin — small, black,
and highly polished — projects from the wall
about four feet, the further end being supported
by what looks like an ornamental black flower-pot
standing on a pedestal. The coffin is the oven,
and the flower-pot is the stove. Given a handful
of small coal or charcoal, Madame appears cap-

able of keeping it at work all day, and of boiling,
baking, or roasting you innumerable dishes.

Then there is the family. Who or what they all
are, and where they all sleep, is a profound mystery. The family tree is usually headed by a de-
crepit and ruminant old gentleman in a species of
yachting-cap. He sits behind the stove — not
exactly with one foot in the grave, but with both
knees well up against the coffin — and occasionally offers a mumbled observation of which no one
takes the slightest notice. Sometimes, too, there
is an old, a very old, lady. Probably she is some
one's grandmother, or great-grandmother, but
she does not appear to be related to the old gentleman. At least, they never recognise one another's
existence in any way.

There are also vague people who possess the
power of becoming invisible at will. They fade in
and out of the house like wraiths: their one object
in life appears to be to efface themselves as much
as possible. Madame refers to them as *"refugiés"*;
this the sophisticated Mr. Cockerell translates,
"German spies."

Next in order come one or two farmhands —
usually addressed as "'Nri!" and "'Seph!" They
are not as a rule either attractive in appearance or
desirable in character. Every man in this country,
who *is* a man, is away, as a matter of course, doing
a man's only possible duty under the circumstances. This leaves 'Nri and 'Seph, who through
physical or mental shortcomings are denied the
proud privilege, and shamble about in the muck
and mud of the farm, leering or grumbling, while

Madame exhorts them to further activity from
the kitchen door. They take their meals with the
family: where they sleep no one knows. External
evidence suggests the cow-house.

Then, the family. First, Angèle. She may be
twenty-five, but is more probably fifteen. She
acts as Adjutant to Madame, and rivals her
mother as deliverer of sustained and rapid recita-
tive. She milks the cows, feeds the pigs, and dra-
goons her young brothers and sisters. But though
she works from morning till night, she has always
time for a smiling salutation to all ranks. She
also speaks English quite creditably — a fact of
which Madame is justly proud. "Collège!" explains the mother, full of appreciation for an education which she herself has never known, and
taps her learned daughter affectionately upon the
head.

Next in order comes Émile. He must be about
fourteen, but War has forced manhood on him.
All day long he is at work, bullying very large
horses, digging, hoeing, even ploughing. He is
very much a boy, for all that. He whistles excru-
ciatingly — usually English music-hall melodies
— grins sheepishly at the officers, and is prepared
at any moment to abandon the most important
tasks, in order to watch a man cleaning a rifle or
oiling a machine-gun. We seem to have encountered Émile in other countries than this.

After Émile, Gabrielle. Her age is probably
seven. If you were to give her a wash and brush-
up, dress her in a gauzy frock, and exchange her
thick woollen stockings and wooden sabots for

silk and dancing slippers, she would make a very smart little fairy. Even in her native state she is a most attractive young person, of an engaging coyness. If you say: "Bonjour, Gabrielle!" she whispers: "B'jour M'sieur le Capitaine" — or, "M'sieur le Caporal"; for she knows all badges of rank — and hangs her head demurely. But presently, if you stand quite still and look the other way, Gabrielle will sidle up to you and squeeze your hand. This is gratifying, but a little subversive of strict discipline if you happen to be inspecting your platoon at the moment.

Gabrielle is a firm favourite with the rank and file. Her particular crony is one Private Mackay, an amorphous youth with flaming red hair. He and Gabrielle engage in lengthy conversations, which appear to be perfectly intelligible to both, though Mackay speaks with the solemn unction of the Aberdonian, and Gabrielle prattles at express speed in a *patois* of her own. Last week some unknown humorist, evidently considering that Gabrielle was not making sufficient progress in her knowledge of English, took upon himself to give her a private lesson. Next morning Mackay, on sentry duty at the farm gate, espied his little friend peeping round a corner.

"Hey, Garibell!" he observed cheerfully. (No Scottish private ever yet mastered a French name quite completely.)

Gabrielle, anxious to exhibit her new accomplishment, drew nearer, smiled seraphically, and replied —

"'Ello, Gingeair!"

Last of the bunch comes Petit Jean, a chubby
and close-cropped youth of about six. Petit Jean
is not his real name, as he himself indignantly explained when so addressed by Major Wagstaffe.

"Moi, z'ne suis pas Petit Jean; z'suis Maurr-
rice!"

Major Wagstaffe apologised most humbly, but
the name stuck.

Petit Jean is an enthusiast upon matters military. He possesses a little wooden rifle, the gift of
a friendly "Écossais," tipped with a flashing bayonet cut from a biscuit-tin; and spends most of his
time out upon the road, waiting for some one to
salute. At one time he used to stand by the sentry, with an ancient glengarry crammed over his
bullet head, and conform meticulously to his com-
rade's slightest movement. This procedure was
soon banned, as being calculated to bring contempt and ridicule upon the King's uniform, and
Petit Jean was assigned a beat of his own. Behold
him upon sentry-go.

A figure upon horseback swings round the bend
in the road.

"Here's an officer, Johnny!" cries a friendly
voice from the farm gate.

Petit Jean, as upright as a post, brings his rifle
from stand-at-ease to the order, and from the order to the slope, with the epileptic jerkiness of a
marionette, and scrutinises the approaching officer
for stars and crowns. If he can discern nothing but
a star or two, he slaps the small of his butt with
ferocious solemnity; but if a crown, or a red hat-
band, reveals itself, he blows out his small chest

to its fullest extent and presents arms. If the salute is acknowledged — as it nearly always is — Petit Jean is crimson with gratification. Once, when a friendly subaltern called his platoon to attention, and gave the order, "Eyes right!" upon passing the motionless little figure at the side of the road, Petit Jean was so uplifted that he committed the military crime of deserting his post while on duty — in order to run home and tell his mother about it.

Last of all we arrive at the keystone of the whole fabric — Madame herself. She is one of the most wonderful women in the world. Consider. Her husband and her eldest son are away — fighting, she knows not where, amid dangers and privations which can only be imagined. During their absence she has to manage a considerable farm, with the help of her children and one or two hired labourers of more than doubtful use or reliability. In addition to her ordinary duties as a parent and *fermière*, she finds herself called upon, for months on end, to maintain her premises as a combination of barracks and almshouse. Yet she is seldom cross — except possibly when the *soldats* steal her apples and pelt the pigs with the cores — and no accumulations of labour can sap her energy. She is up by half-past four every morning; yet she never appears anxious to go to bed at night. The last sound which sleepy subalterns hear is Madame's voice, uplifted in steady discourse to the circle round the stove, sustained by an occasional guttural chord from 'Nri and 'Seph. She has been

doing this, day in, day out, since the combatants
settled down to trench-warfare. Every few weeks
brings a fresh crop of tenants, with fresh peculiari-
ties and unknown proclivities; and she assimilates
them all.

The only approach to a breakdown comes
when, after paying her little bill — you may be
sure that not an omelette nor a broken window
will be missing from the account — and wishing
her "Bonne chance!" ere you depart, you venture
on a reference, in a few awkward, stumbling sentences, to the absent husband and son. Then she
weeps, copiously, and it seems to do her a world of
good. All hail to you, Madame — the finest ex-
ponent, in all this War, of the art of Carrying On!
We know now why France is such a great country.

VI

I

PRACTICALLY all the business of an Army in the field is transacted by telephone. If the telephone breaks down, whether by the Act of God or of the King's Enemies, that business is at a standstill until the telephone is put right again.

The importance of the disaster varies with the nature of the business. For instance, if the wire leading to the Round Game Department is blown down by a March gale, and your weekly return of Men Recommended for False Teeth is delayed in transit, nobody minds very much — except possibly the Deputy Assistant Director of Auxiliary Dental Appliances. But if you are engaged in battle, and the wires which link up the driving force in front with the directing force behind are devastated by a storm of shrapnel, the matter assumes a more — nay, a most — serious aspect. Hence the superlative importance in modern warfare of the Signal Sections of the Royal Engineers — tersely described by the rank-and-file as the "Buzzers," or the "Iddy-Umpties."

During peace-training, the Buzzer on the whole has a very pleasant time of it. Once he has mastered the mysteries of the Semaphore and Morse codes, the most laborious part of his education is over. Henceforth he spends his days upon some sheltered hillside, in company with one or two congenial spirits, flapping cryptic messages out of a blue-and-white flag at a similar party across the valley.

A year ago, for instance, you might have encountered an old friend, Private M'Micking, — one of the original "Buzzers" of "A" Company, and ultimately Battalion Signal Sergeant — under the lee of a pine wood near Hindhead, accompanied by Lance-Corporal Greig and Private Wamphray, regarding with languid interest the frenzied efforts of three of their colleagues to convey a message from a sunny hillside three quarters of a mile away.

"Here a message comin' through, boys," announces the Lance-Corporal. "They're in a sair hurry: I doot the officer will be there. Jeams, tak' it doon while Sandy reads it."

Mr. James M'Micking seats himself upon a convenient log. In order not to confuse his faculties by endeavouring to read and write simultaneously, he turns his back upon the fluttering flag, and bends low over his field message-pad. Private Wamphray stands facing him, and solemnly spells out the message over his head.

"Tae g-o-c — I dinna ken what that means — r-e-d, *reid* — a-r-m-y, *airmy* — h-a-z —"

"All richt; that 'll be Haslemere," says Private M'Micking, scribbling down the word. "Go on, Sandy!"

Private Wamphray, pausing to expectorate, continues —

"R-e-c-o-n-n-o-i-t-r — Cricky, what a worrd!
Let's hae it repeatit."

Wamphray flaps his flag vigorously, — he
knows this particular signal only too well, — and
the word comes through again. The distant signaller, slowing down a little, continues, —

"'Reconnoitring patrol reports hostile cavalry
scou —'"

"That'll be 'scouts,'" says the ever-ready
M'Micking. "Carry on!"

Wamphray continues obediently, —

"'Country'; stop; 'Have thrown out flank
guns'; stop; 'Shall I advance or re —'"

"— tire," gabbles M'Micking, writing it down.

· "— 'where I am'; stop; 'From O C Advance
Guard'; stop; message ends."

"And aboot time, too!" observes the scribe
severely. "Haw, Johnny!"

The Lance-Corporal, who has been indulging in
a pleasant reverie upon a bank of bracken, wakes
up and reads the proffered message.

"Tae G O C, Reid Airmy, Hazlemere. Reconnoitring patrol reports hostile cavalry scouts
country. Have thrown oot flank guns. Shall I
advance or retire where I am? From O C Advance
Guard."

"This message doesna sound altogether sense,"
he observes mildly. "That 'shall' should be
'wull,' onyway. Would it no' be better to get it
repeatit? The officer —"

"I've given the 'message-read' signal now,"
objects the indolent Wamphray.

"How would it be," suggests the Lance-Corporal, whose besetting sin is a *penchant* for emendation, "if we were tae transfair yon stop, and say: 'Reconnoitring patrol reports hostile cavalry scouts. Country has thrown oot flank guns'?"

"What does that mean?" inquires M'Micking scornfully.

"I dinna ken; but these messages about Generals and sic'-like bodies —"

At this moment, as ill-luck will have it, the Signal Sergeant appears breasting the hillside. He arrives puffing — he has seen twenty years' service — and scrutinises the message.

"You boys," he says reproachfully, "are an aggravate altogether. Here you are, jumping at your conclusions again! After all I have been telling you! See! That worrd in the address should no' be Haslemere at all. It's just a catch! It's Hazebroucke — a Gairman city that we'll be capturing this time next year. 'Scouts' is no 'scouts,' but 'scouring' — meaning 'sooping up.' 'Guns' should be 'guarrd,' and 'retire' should be 'remain.' Mind me, now; next time, you'll be up before the Captain for neglect of duty. Wamphray, give the 'C.I.,' and let's get hame to oor dinners!"

II

But "oot here" there is no flag-wagging. The Buzzer's first proceeding upon entering the field of active hostilities is to get underground, and stay there.

He is a seasoned vessel, the Buzzer of to-day,

and a person of marked individuality. He is
above all things a man of the world. Sitting day
and night in a dug-out, or a cellar, with a telephone receiver clamped to his ear, he sees little;
but he hears much, and overhears more. He also
speaks a language of his own. His one task in life
is to prevent the letter B from sounding like C, or
D, or P, or T, or V, over the telephone; so he has
perverted the English language to his own uses.
He calls B "Beer," and D "Don," and so on. He
salutes the rosy dawn as "Akk Emma," and even-
tide as "Pip Emma." He refers to the letter S as
"Esses," in order to distinguish it from F. He has
no respect for the most majestic military titles.
To him the Deputy Assistant Director of the
Mobile Veterinary Section is merely a lifeless formula, entitled Don Akk Don Emma Vic Esses.

He is also a man of detached mind. The tactical
situation does not interest him. His business is to
disseminate news, not to write leading articles
about it. (*O si sic omnes!*) You may be engaged
in a life-and-death struggle for the possession of
your own parapet with a Boche bombing-party;
but this does not render you immune from a pink
slip from the Signal Section, asking you to state
your reasons in writing for having mislaid fourteen pairs of "boots, gum, thigh," lately the
property of Number Seven Platoon. A famous
British soldier tells a story somewhere in his remi-
niscences of an occasion upon which, in some long-
forgotten bush campaign, he had to defend a
zareba against a heavy attack. For a time the
situation was critical. Help was badly needed,

but the telegraph wire had been cut. Ultimately the attack withered away, and the situation was saved. Almost simultaneously the victorious commander was informed that telegraphic communication with the Base had been restored. A message was already coming through.

"News of reinforcements, I hope!" he remarked to his subordinate.

But his surmise was incorrect. The message said, quite simply: —

"Your monthly return of men wishing to change their religion is twenty-four hours overdue. Please expedite."

There was a time when one laughed at that anecdote as a playful invention. But we know now that it is true, and we feel a sort of pride in the truly British imperturbability of our official machinery.

Thirdly, the Buzzer is a humourist, of the sardonic variety. The constant clash of wits over the wires, and the necessity of framing words quickly, sharpens his faculties and acidulates his tongue. Incidentally, he is an awkward person to quarrel with. One black night, Bobby Little, making his second round of the trenches about an hour before "stand-to," felt constrained to send a telephone message to Battalion Headquarters. Taking a good breath, — you always do this before entering a trench dug-out, — he plunged into the noisome cavern where his Company Signallers kept everlasting vigil. The place was in total

darkness, except for the illumination supplied by
a strip of rifle-rag burning in a tin of rifle-oil. The
air, what there was of it, was thick with large,
fat, floating particles of free carbon. The telephone was buzzing plaintively to itself, in unsuccessful competition with a well-modulated quartette for four nasal organs, contributed by Bobby's
entire signalling staff, who, locked in the inex-
tricable embrace peculiar to Thomas Atkins in
search of warmth, were snoring harmoniously
upon the earthen floor.

The signaller "on duty" — one M'Gurk — was
extracted from the heap and put under arrest for
sleeping at his post. The enormity of his crime
was heightened by the fact that two undelivered
messages were found upon his person.

Divers pains and penalties followed. Bobby
supplemented the sentence with a homily on the
importance of vigilance and despatch. M'Gurk,
deeply aggrieved at forfeiting seven days' pay,
said nothing, but bided his time. Two nights later the Battalion came out of trenches for a week's
rest, and Bobby, weary and thankful, retired to
bed in his hut at 9 P.M., in comfortable anticipa-
tion of a full night's repose.

His anticipations were doomed to disappoint-
ment. He was roused from slumber — not without difficulty — by Signaller M'Gurk, who appeared standing by his bedside with a guttering
candle-end in one hand and a pink despatch-form
in the other. The message said: —

"Prevailing wind for next twenty-four hours
probably S.W., with some rain."

Mindful of his own recent admonitions, Bobby thanked M'Gurk politely, and went to sleep again.

M'Gurk called again at half-past two in the morning, with another message, which announced: —

"Baths will be available for your Company from 2 to 3 P.M. to-morrow."

Bobby stuffed the missive under his air-pillow, and rolled over without a word. M'Gurk withdrew, leaving the door of the hut open.

His next visit was about four o'clock. This time the message said: —

"A Zeppelin is reported to have passed over Dunkirk at 5 P.M. yesterday afternoon, proceeding in a northerly direction."

Bobby informed M'Gurk that he was a fool and a dotard, and cast him forth.

M'Gurk returned at five-thirty, bearing written evidence that the Zeppelin had been traced as far as Ostend.

This time his Company Commander promised him that if he appeared again that night he would be awarded fourteen days' Field Punishment Number One.

The result was that upon sitting down to breakfast at nine next morning, Bobby found upon his plate yet another message — from his Commanding Officer — summoning him to the Orderly-room on urgent matters at eight-thirty.

But Bobby scored the final and winning trick. Sending for M'Gurk and Sergeant M'Micking, he said: —

"This man, Sergeant, appears to be unable to

decide when a message is urgent and when it is
not. In future, whenever M'Gurk is on night
duty, and is in doubt as to whether a message
should be delivered at once or put aside till morning, he will come to you and ask for your guidance
in the matter. Do you understand?"

"Perrfectly, sirr!" replied the Sergeant, out-
wardly calm.

"M'Gurk, do *you* understand?"

M'Gurk looked at Bobby, and then round at
Sergeant M'Micking. He received a glance which
shrivelled his marrow. The game was up. He
grinned sheepishly, and answered, —

"Yis, sirr!"

III

Having briefly set forth the character and
habits of the Buzzer, we will next proceed to visit
the creature in his lair. This is an easy feat. We
have only to walk up the communication-trench
which leads from the reserve line to the firing-line.
Upon either side of the trench, neatly tacked to
the muddy wall by a device of the hairpin variety,
run countless insulated wires, clad in coats of
various colours and all duly ticketed. These radi-
ate from various Headquarters in the rear to numerous signal stations in the front, and were laid
by the Signallers themselves. (It is perhaps unnecessary to mention that that single wire running, in defiance of all regulations, across the top
of the trench, which neatly tipped your cap off
just now, was laid by those playful humourists,
the Royal Artillery.) It follows that if we accom-

pany these wires far enough we shall ultimately find ourselves in a signalling station.

Our only difficulty lies in judicious choice, for the wires soon begin to diverge up numerous by-ways. Some go to the fire-trench, others to the machine-guns, others again to observation posts — or O.P.'s — whence a hawk-eyed Forward Observing Officer, peering all day through a chink in a tumble-down chimney or sandbagged loop-hole, is sometimes enabled to flash back the intelligence that he can discern transport upon such a road in rear of the Boche trenches, and will such a battery kindly attend to the matter at once?

However, chance guides us to the Signal dug-out of "A" Company, where, by the best fortune in the world, Private M'Gurk in person is installed as officiating sprite. Let us render ourselves invisible, sit down beside him, and "tap" his wire.

In the dim and distant days before such phrases as "Boche," and "T.N.T.," and "munitions," and "economy" were invented; when we lived in houses which possessed roofs, and never dreamed of lying down motionless by the roadside when we heard a taxi-whistle blown thrice, in order to escape the notice of approaching aeroplanes, — in short, in the days immediately preceding the war, — some of us said in our haste that the London Telephone Service was The Limit! Since then we have made the acquaintance of the military field-telephone, and we feel distinctly softened towards the young woman at home who, from her dug-out in "Gerrard," or "Vic.," or "Hop.," used to goad

us to impotent frenzy. She was at least terse and
decided. If you rang her up and asked for a number, she merely replied, —

(a) "Number engaged";

(b) "No reply";

(c) "Out of order" —

as the case might be, and switched you off.
After that you took a taxi to the place with which
you wished to communicate, and there was an end
of the matter. Above all, she never explained, she
never wrangled, she spoke tolerably good English,
and there was only one of her — or at least she
was of a uniform type.

Now, if you put your ear to the receiver of a
field-telephone, you find yourself, as it were, suddenly thrust into a vast subterranean cavern,
filled with the wailings of the lost, the babblings of
the feeble-minded, and the profanity of the exas-
perated. If you ask a high-caste Buzzer — say, an
R.E. Signalling Officer — why this should be so,
he will look intensely wise and recite some solemn
gibberish about earthed wires and induced cur-
rents.

The noises are of two kinds, and one supple-
ments the other. The human voice supplies the
libretto, while the accompaniment is provided by
a syncopated and tympanum-piercing *ping-ping*,
suggestive of a giant mosquito singing to its
young.

The instrument with which we are contending
is capable (in theory) of transmitting a message
either telephonically or telegraphically. In practice, this means that the signaller, having wasted

ten sulphurous minutes in a useless attempt to
convey information through the medium of the
human voice, next proceeds, upon the urgent advice of the gentleman at the other end, and to the
confusion of all other inhabitants of the cavern,
to "buzz" it, employing the dots and dashes of
the Morse code for the purpose.

It is believed that the wily Boche, by means of
ingenious and delicate instruments, is able to
"tap" a certain number of our trench telephone
messages. If he does, his daily Intelligence Report must contain some surprising items of information. At the moment when we attach our
invisible apparatus to Mr. M'Gurk's wire, the
Divisional Telephone system appears to be fairly
evenly divided between —

(1) A Regimental Headquarters endeavouring
to ring up its Brigade.

(2) A glee-party of Harmonious Blacksmiths,
indulging in the Anvil Chorus.

(3) A choleric Adjutant on the track of a
peccant Company Commander.

(4) Two Company Signallers, engaged in a
friendly chat from different ends of the trench
line.

(5) An Artillery F.O.O., endeavouring to convey pressing and momentous information to his
Battery, two miles in rear.

(6) The Giant Mosquito aforesaid.

The consolidated result is something like
this: —

REGIMENTAL HEADQUARTERS (*affably*). Hallo,
Brigade! Hallo, Brigade! HALLO, BRIGADE!

THE MOSQUITO. Ping!

THE ADJUTANT (*from somewhere in the Support Line, fiercely*). Give me B Company!

THE FORWARD OBSERVING OFFICER (*from his eyrie*). Is that C Battery? There's an enemy working-party —

FIRST CHATTY SIGNALLER (*from B Company's Station*). Is that yoursel', Jock? How's a' wi' you?

SECOND CHATTY SIGNALLER (*from D Company's Station*). I'm daen fine! How's your —

· REGIMENTAL HEADQUARTERS. HALLO, BRIGADE!

THE ADJUTANT. Is that B Company?

A MYSTERIOUS AND DISTANT VOICE (*politely*). No, sir; this is Akk and Esses Aitch.

THE ADJUTANT (*furiously*). Then for the Lord's sake get off the line!

THE MOSQUITO. Ping! Ping!

THE ADJUTANT. And stop that —— —— ——— buzzing!

THE MOSQUITO. Ping! *Ping!* PING!

THE F.O.O. Is that C Battery? There's —

FIRST CHATTY SIGNALLER (*peevishly*). What's that you're sayin'?

THE F.O.O. (*perseveringly*). Is that C Battery? There's an enemy working-party in a coppice at —

FIRST CHATTY SIGNALLER. This is Beer Company, sir. Weel, Jock, did ye get a quiet nicht?

SECOND CHATTY SIGNALLER. Oh, aye. There was a wee —

THE F.O.O. Is that C Battery? There's —

SECOND CHATTY SIGNALLER. No, sir. This is
Don Company. Weel, Jimmy, there was a
couple whish-bangs came intil —

REGIMENTAL HEADQUARTERS. HALLO, BRI-
GADE!

A CHEERFUL COCKNEY VOICE. Well, my lad,
what abaht it?

REGIMENTAL HEADQUARTERS (*getting to work at
once*). Hold the line, Brigade. Message to Staff
Captain. "Ref. your S.C. fourr stroke seeven
eight six, the worrking-parrty in question —"

THE F.O.O. (*seeing a gleam of hope*). Working-
party? Is that C Battery? I want to speak to —

THE ADJUTANT. ⎫
BRIGADE HEADQUARTERS. ⎬ Get off the
REGIMENTAL HEADQUARTERS. ⎭ line!

FIRST CHATTY SIGNALLER. Haw, Jock, was ye
hearin' aboot Andra?

SECOND CHATTY SIGNALLER. No. Whit was
that?

FIRST CHATTY SIGNALLER. Weel —

THE F.O.O. (*doggedly*). Is that C Battery?

REGIMENTAL HEADQUARTERS (*resolutely*). "The
worrking-parrty in question was duly detailed for
tae proceed to the rendiss vowse at" —

THE ADJUTANT. Is that B Company, curse
you?

REGIMENTAL HEADQUARTERS (*quite impervious
to this sort of thing*), — "the rendiss vowse, at
seeven thirrty Akk Emma, at point H two B
eight nine, near the cross-roads by the Estamint
Repose dee Bicyclistees, for tae" — honk! honkle!
honk!

BRIGADE HEADQUARTERS (*compassionately*). You're makin' a 'orrible mess of this message, ain't you? Shake your transmitter, do!

REGIMENTAL HEADQUARTERS (*after dutifully performing this operation*). Honkle, honkle, honk. Yang!

BRIGADE HEADQUARTERS. Buzz it, my lad, buzz it!

REGIMENTAL HEADQUARTERS (*dutifully*). Ping, ping! Ping, ping! Ping, ping, ping! Ping —

GENERAL CHORUS. Stop that ——, ——, ——, —— buzzing!

FIRST CHATTY SIGNALLER. Weel, Andra says tae the Sergeant-Major of Beer Company, says he —

THE ADJUTANT. Is that B Company?

FIRST CHATTY SIGNALLER. No, sir; this is Beer Company.

THE ADJUTANT (*fortissimo*). I *said* Beer Company!

FIRST CHATTY SIGNALLER. Oh! I thocht ye meant Don Company, sir.

THE ADJUTANT. Why the blazes have n't you answered me sooner?

FIRST CHATTY SIGNALLER (*tactfully*). There was other messages comin' through, sir.

THE ADJUTANT. Well, get me the Company Commander.

FIRST CHATTY SIGNALLER. Varra good, sirr.

A pause. Regimental Headquarters being engaged in laboriously "buzzing" its message through to the Brigade, all other conversation is at a standstill. The Harmonious Blacksmiths seize the opportunity to give a short selection. Presently, as the din dies down —

THE F.O.O. (*faint, yet pursuing*). Is that C Battery?

A JOVIAL VOICE. Yes.

THE F.O.O. What a shock! I thought you were all dead. Is that you, Chumps?

THE JOVIAL VOICE. It is. What can I do for you this morning?

THE F.O.O. You can boil your signal sentry's head!

THE JOVIAL VOICE. What for?

THE F.O.O. For keeping me waiting.

THE JOVIAL VOICE. Righto! And the next article?

THE F.O.O. There's a Boche working-party in a coppice two hundred yards west of a point —

THE MOSQUITO (*with renewed vigour*). Ping, ping!

THE F.O.O. (*savagely*). Shut up!

THE JOVIAL VOICE. Working-party? I'll settle them. What's the map reference?

THE F.O.O. They are in Square number —

THE HARMONIOUS BLACKSMITHS (*suddenly and stunningly*). Whang!

THE F.O.O. Shut up! They are in Square —

FIRST CHATTY SIGNALLER. Hallo, Headquarters! Is the Adjutant there? Here's the Captain tae speak with him.

AN EAGER VOICE. Is that the Adjutant?

REGIMENTAL HEADQUARTERS. No, sirr. He's away tae his office. Hold the line while I'll —

THE EAGER VOICE. No you don't! Put me

straight through to C Battery — quick! Then
get off the line, and stay there! (*Much buzzing.*)
Is that C Battery?

THE JOVIAL VOICE. Yes, sir.

THE EAGER VOICE. I am O.C. Beer Company.
They are shelling my front parapet, at L 8, with
pretty heavy stuff. I want retaliation, please.

THE JOVIAL VOICE. Very good, sir. (*The voice
dies away.*)

A SOUND OVER OUR HEADS (*thirty seconds later*).
Whish! Whish! Whish!

SECOND CHATTY SIGNALLER. Did ye hear that,
Jimmy?

FIRST CHATTY SIGNALLER (*with relish*). Mphm!
That'll sorrt them!

THE F.O.O. Is that C Battery?

THE JOVIAL VOICE. Yes. What luck, old son?

THE F.O.O. You have obtained two direct hits
on the Boche parapet. Will you have a cocoanut
or a ci——

THE JOVIAL VOICE. A little less lip, my lad!
Now tell me all about your industrious friends in
the Coppice, and we will see what we can do for
them!

And so on. Apropos of Adjutants and Company Commanders, Private Wamphray, whose
acquaintance we made a few pages back, was ultimately relieved of his position as a Company Signaller, and returned ignominiously to duty, for
tactless if justifiable interposition in one of these
very dialogues.

It was a dark and cheerless night in mid-winter.

Ominous noises in front of the Boche wire had raised apprehensive surmises in the breast of Brigade Headquarters. A forward sap was suspected in the region opposite the sector of trenches held by "A" Company. The trenches at this point were barely forty yards apart, and there was a very real danger that Brother Boche might creep under his own wire, and possibly under ours too, and come tumbling over our parapet.

To Bobby Little came instructions to send a specially selected patrol out to investigate the matter. Three months ago he would have led the expedition himself. Now, as a full-blown Company Commander, he was officially precluded from exposing his own most responsible person to gratuitous risks. So he chose out that recently-joined enthusiast, Angus M'Lachlan, and put him over the parapet on the dark night in question, accompanied by Corporal M'Snape and two scouts, with orders to probe the mystery to its depth and bring back a full report.

It was a ticklish enterprise. As is frequently the case upon these occasions, nervous tension manifested itself much more seriously at Headquarters than in the front-line trenches. The man on the spot is, as a rule, much too busy with the actual execution of the enterprise in hand to distress himself by speculation upon its ultimate outcome. It may as well be stated at once that Angus duly returned from his quest, with an admirable and reassuring report. But he was a long time absent. Hence this anecdote.

Bobby had strict orders to report all "develop-

ments," as they occurred, to Headquarters by
telephone. At half-past eleven that night, as
Angus M'Lachlan's colossal form disappeared,
crawling, into the blackness of night, his superior
officer dutifully rang up Battalion Headquarters,
and announced that the venture was launched.
It is possible that the Powers Behind were in possession of information as to the enemy's inten-
tions unrevealed to Bobby; for as soon as his opening announcement was received, he was switched
right through to a very august Headquarters indeed, and commanded to report direct.

Long-distance telephony in the field involves
a considerable amount of "linking-up." Among
other slaves of the Buzzer who assisted in estab-
lishing the necessary communications upon this
occasion was Private Wamphray. For the next
hour and a half it was his privilege in his subterranean exchange, to sit, with his receiver clamped
to his ear, an unappreciative auditor of dialogues
like the following: —

"Is that 'A' Company?"

"Yes, sir."

"Any news of your patrol?"

"No, sir."

Again, five minutes later: —

"Is that 'A' Company?"

"Yes, sir."

"Has your officer returned yet?"

"No, sir. I will notify you when he does."

This sort of thing went on until nearly one
o'clock in the morning. Towards that hour,
Bobby, who was growing really concerned over

Angus's prolonged absence, cut short his august interlocutor's fifteenth inquiry and joined his Sergeant-Major on the firing-step. The two had hardly exchanged a few low-pitched sentences when Bobby was summoned back to the telephone.

"Is that Captain Little?"

"Yes, sir."

"Has your patrol come in?"

"No, sir."

Captain's Little's last answer was delivered in a distinctly insubordinate manner. Feeling slightly relieved, he returned to the firing-step. Two minutes later Angus M'Lachlan and his posse rolled over the parapet, safe and sound, and Bobby was able, to his own great content and that of the weary operators along the line, to announce, —

"The patrol has returned, sir, and reports everything quite satisfactory. I am forwarding a detailed statement."

Then he laid down the receiver with a happy sigh, and crawled out of the dug-out on to the duck-board.

"Now we'll have a look round the sentries, Sergeant-Major," he said.

But the pair had hardly rounded three traverses when Bobby was haled back to the Signal Station.

"Why did you leave the telephone just now?" inquired a cold voice.

"I was going to visit my sentries, sir."

"But *I* was speaking to you."

"I thought you had finished, sir."

"I had *not* finished. If I had finished, I should have informed you of the fact, and would have said 'Good-night!'"

"How *does* one choke off a tripe-merchant of this type?" wondered the exhausted officer.

From the bowels of the earth came the answer to his unspoken question — delivered in a strong Paisley accent —

"For Goad's sake, kiss him, and *say* 'Good-Nicht,' and hae done with it!"

As already stated, Private Wamphray was returned to his platoon next morning.

IV

But to regard the Buzzer simply and solely as a troglodyte, of sedentary habits and caustic temperament, is not merely hopelessly wrong: it is grossly unjust. Sometimes he goes for a walk — under some such circumstances as the following.

The night is as black as Tartarus, and it is raining heavily. Brother Boche, a prey to nervous qualms, is keeping his courage up by distributing shrapnel along our communication-trenches. Signal-wires are peculiarly vulnerable to shrapnel. Consequently no one in the Battalion Signal Station is particularly surprised when the line to "Akk" Company suddenly ceases to perform its functions.

Signal-Sergeant M'Micking tests the instrument, glances over his shoulder, and observes, —

"Line BX is gone, some place or other. Away you, Duncan, and sorrt it!"

Mr. Duncan, who has been sitting hunched over a telephone, temporarily quiescent, smoking a woodbine, heaves a resigned sigh, extinguishes the woodbine and places it behind his ear; hitches his repairing-wallet nonchalantly over his shoulder, and departs into the night — there to grope in several inches of mud for the two broken ends of the wire, which may be lying fifty yards apart. Having found them, he proceeds to effect a junction, his progress being impeded from time to time by further bursts of shrapnel. This done, he tests the new connection, relights his woodbine, and splashes his way back to Headquarters. That is a Buzzer's normal method of obtaining fresh air and exercise.

More than that. He is the one man in the Army who can fairly describe himself as indispensable.

In these days, when whole nations are deployed against one another, no commander, however eminent, can ride the whirlwind single-handed. There are limits to individual capacity. There are limits to direct control. There are limits to personal magnetism. We fight upon a collective plan nowadays. If we propose to engage in battle, we begin by welding a hundred thousand men into one composite giant. We weld a hundred thousand rifles, a million bombs, a thousand machine-guns, and as many pieces of artillery, into one huge weapon of offence, with which we arm our giant. Having done this, we provide him with a brain — a blend of all the experience and wisdom and military genius at our disposal. But still there is one thing lacking — a nervous system.

Unless our giant have that, — unless his brain be
able to transmit its desires to his mighty limbs, —
he has nothing. He is of no account; the enemy
can make butcher's-meat of him. And that is why
I say that the purveyor of this nervous system —
our friend the Buzzer — is indispensable. You can
always create a body of sorts and a brain of sorts.
But unless you can produce a nervous system of the
highest excellence, you are foredoomed to failure.

Take a small instance. Supposing a battalion
advances to the attack, and storms an isolated,
exposed position. Can they hold on, or can they
not? That question can only be answered by the
Artillery behind them. If the curtain of shell-fire
which has preceded the advancing battalion to its
objective can be "lifted" at the right moment and
put down again, with precision, upon a certain
vital zone beyond the captured line, counter-
attacks can be broken up and the line held. But
the Artillery lives a long way — sometimes miles
— in rear. Without continuous and accurate information it will be more than useless; it will
be dangerous. (A successful attacking party has
been shelled out of its hardly won position by its
own artillery before now — on both sides!) Sometimes a little visual signalling is possible: sometimes a despatch-runner may get back through
the enemy's curtain of fire; but in the main your
one hope of salvation hangs upon a slender thread
of insulated wire. And round that wire are strung
some of the purest gems of heroism that the War
has produced.

At the Battle of Loos, half a battalion of

"K (1)" pushed forward into a very advanced
hostile position. There they hung, by their teeth.
Their achievement was great; but unless Headquarters could be informed of their exact position
and needs, they were all dead men. So Corporal
Greig set out to find them, unreeling wire as he
went. He was blown to pieces by an eight-inch
shell, but another signaller was never lacking to
take his place. They pressed forward, these lacka-
daisical noncombatants, until the position was
reached and communication established. Again
and again the wire was cut by shrapnel, and again
and again a Buzzer crawled out to find the broken
ends and piece them together. And ultimately,
the tiny, exposed limb in front having been enabled to explain its exact requirements to the
brain behind, the necessary help was forthcoming
and the Fort was held.

Next time you pass a Signaller's Dug-out peep
inside. You will find it occupied by a coke brazier,
emitting large quantities of carbon monoxide, and
an untidy gentleman in khaki, with a blue-and-
white device upon his shoulder-straps, who is
humped over a small black instrument, luxuriat-
ing in a "frowst" most indescribable. He is reading a back number of a rural Scottish newspaper
which you never heard of. Occasionally, in response to a faint buzz, he takes up his transmitter
and indulges in an unintelligible altercation with
a person unseen. You need feel no surprise if he
is wearing the ribbon of the Distinguished Conduct Medal.

VII

PASTURES NEW

I

THE outstanding feature of to-day's intelligence is that spring is coming — has come, in fact.

It arrived with a bump. March entered upon its second week with seven degrees of frost and four inches of snow. We said what was natural and inevitable to the occasion, wrapped our coats of skins more firmly round us, and made a point of attending punctually when the rum ration was issued.

Forty-eight hours later winter had disappeared. The sun was blazing in a cloudless sky. Aeroplanes were battling for photographic rights overhead; the brown earth beneath our feet was putting forth its first blades of tender green. The muck-heap outside our rest-billet displayed unmistakable signs of upheaval from its winter sleep. Primroses appeared in Bunghole Wood; larks soared up into the sky above No Man's Land, making music for the just and the unjust. Snipers, smiling cheerfully over the improved atmospheric conditions, polished up their telescopic sights. The artillery on each side hailed the birth of yet another season of fruitfulness and natural increase with some more than usually enthusiastic essays in mutual extermination. Half the Mess caught colds in their heads.

Frankly, we are not sorry to see the end of winter. Cæsar, when he had concluded his summer campaign, went into winter quarters. Cæsar, as Colonel Kemp once huskily remarked, knew something!

Still, each man to his taste. Corporal Mucklewame, for one, greatly prefers winter to summer.

"In the winter," he points out to Sergeant M'Snape, "a body can breathe withoot swallowing a wheen bluebottles and bum-bees. A body can aye streitch himself doon under a tree for a bit sleep withoot getting wasps and wee beasties crawling up inside his kilt, and puddocks craw-crawing in his ear! A body can keep himself frae sweitin' —"

"He can that!" assents M'Snape, whose spare frame is more vulnerable to the icy breeze than that of the stout corporal.

However, the balance of public opinion is against Mucklewame. Most of us are unfeignedly glad to feel the warmth of the sun again. That working-party, filling sandbags just behind the machine-gun emplacement, are actually singing. Spring gets into the blood, even in this stricken land. The Boche over the way resents our efforts at harmony.

> Sing us a song, a song of Bonnie Scotland!
>   Any old song will do.
> By the old camp-fire, the rough-and-ready choir
>   Join in the chorus too.
> "You'll tak' the high road and I'll tak' the low road" —
>   'T is a song that we all know,
> To bring back the days in Bonnie Scotland,
>   Where the heather and the bluebells —

Whang!

The Boche, a Wagnerian by birth and upbringing, cannot stand any more of this, so he has fired a rifle-grenade at the glee-party — on the whole a much more honest and direct method of condemnation than that practiced by musical critics in time of peace. But he only elicits an encore. Private Nigg perches a steel helmet on the point of a bayonet, and patronisingly bobs the same up and down above the parapet.

These steel helmets have not previously been introduced to the reader's notice. They are modelled upon those worn in the French Army — and bear about as much resemblance to the original pattern as a Thames barge to a racing yacht. When first issued, they were greeted with profound suspicion. Though undoubtedly serviceable, — they saved many a crown from cracking round The Bluff the other day, — they were undeniably heavy, and they were certainly not becoming to the peculiar type of beauty rampant in "K (1)." On issue, then, their recipients elected to regard the wearing of them as a peculiarly noxious form of "fatigue." Private M'A. deposited his upon the parapet, like a foundling on a doorstep, and departed stealthily round the nearest traverse, to report his new headpiece "lost through the exigencies of military service." Private M'B. wore his insecurely perched upon the top of his tam-o'-shanter bonnet, where it looked like a very large ostrich egg in a very small khaki nest. Private M'C. set his up on a convenient post, and opened rapid fire upon it at a range

of six yards, surveying the resulting holes with
the gloomy satisfaction of the vindicated pes-
simist. Private M'D. removed the lining from
his, and performed his ablutions in the inverted
crown.

"This," said Colonel Kemp, "will never do.
We must start wearing the dashed things ourselves."

And it was so. Next day, to the joy of the Battalion, their officers appeared in the trenches self-
consciously wearing what looked like small sky-
blue wash-hand basins balanced upon their heads.
But discipline was excellent. No one even smiled.
In fact, there was a slight reaction in favour of the
helmets. Conversations like the following were
overheard: —

"I'm tellin' you, Jimmy, the C.O. is no the
man for tae mak' a show of himself like that for
naething. These tin bunnets must be some use.
Wull we pit oors on?"

"Awa' hame, and bile your heid!" replied the
unresponsive James.

"They'll no stop a whish-bang," conceded the
apostle of progress, "but they would keep off
splunters, and a wheen bullets, and — and —"

"And the rain!" supplied Jimmy sarcastically.

This gibe suddenly roused the temper of the
other participant in the debate.

"I tell you," he exclaimed, in a voice shrill with
indignation, "that these —— helmets are some
—— use!"

"And I tell *you*," retorted James earnestly,
"that these —— helmets are no —— —— use!"

When two reasonable persons arrive at a controversial *impasse*, they usually agree to differ and go their several ways. But in "K (1)" we prefer practical solutions. The upholder of helmets hastily thrust his upon his head.

"I'll show you, Jimmy!" he announced, and clambered up on the firing-step.

"And I'll —— well show *you*, Wullie!" screamed James, doing likewise.

Simultaneously the two zealots thrust their heads over the parapet, and awaited results. These came. The rifles of two Boche snipers rang out, and both demonstrators fell heavily backwards into the arms of their supporters.

By all rights they ought to have been killed. But they were both very much alive. Each turned to the other triumphantly, and exclaimed, —

"I tellt ye so!"

There was a hole right through the helmet of Jimmy, the unbeliever. The fact that there was not also a hole through his head was due to his forethought in having put on a tam-o'-shanter underneath. The net result was a truncated "toorie." Wullie's bullet had struck his helmet at a more obtuse angle, and had glanced off, as the designer of the smooth exterior had intended it to do.

At first glance, the contest was a draw. But subsequent investigation elicited the fact that Jimmy in his backward fall had bitten his tongue to the effusion of blood. The verdict was therefore awarded, on points, to Wullie, and the spectators dispersed in an orderly manner just as the platoon sergeant came round the traverse to change the sentry.

II

We have occupied our own present trenches since January. There was a time when this sector of the line was regarded as a Vale of Rest. Bishops were conducted round with impunity. Members of Parliament came out for the week-end, and returned to their constituents with first-hand information about the horrors of war. Foreign journalists, and sight-seeing parties of munition-workers, picnicked in Bunghole Wood. In the village behind the line, if a chance shell removed tiles from the roof of a house, the owner, greatly incensed, mounted a ladder and put in some fresh ones.

But that is all over now. "K (1)"—hard-headed men of business, bountifully endowed with munitions — have arrived upon the scene, and the sylvan peace of the surrounding district is gone. Pan has dug himself in.

The trouble began two months ago, when our Divisional Artillery arrived. Unversed in local etiquette, they commenced operations by "sending up" — to employ a vulgar but convenient catch-phrase — a strongly fortified farmhouse in the enemy's support line. The Boche, by way of gentle reproof, deposited four or five small "whizz-bangs" in our front-line trenches. The tenants thereof promptly telephoned to "Mother," and Mother came to the assistance of her offspring with a salvo of twelve-inch shells. After that,

Brother Boche, realising that the golden age was past, sent north to the Salient for a couple of heavy batteries, and settled down to shell Bunghole village to pieces. Within a week he had brought down the church tower: within a fortnight the population had migrated farther back, leaving behind a few patriots, too deeply interested in the sale of small beer and picture postcards to uproot themselves. Company Headquarters in Bunghole Wood ceased to grow primroses and began to fill sandbags.

A month ago the village was practically intact. The face of the church tower was badly scarred, but the houses were undamaged. The little shops were open; children played in the streets. Now, if you stand at the cross-roads where the church rears its roofless walls, you will understand what the Abomination of Desolation means. Occasionally a body of troops, moving in small detachments at generous intervals, trudges by, on its way to or from the trenches. Occasionally a big howitzer shell swings lazily out of the blue and drops with a crash or a dull thud — according to the degree of resistance encountered — among the crumbling cottages. All is solitude.

But stay! Right on the cross-roads, in the centre of the village, just below the fingers of a sign-post which indicates the distance to four French townships, whose names you never heard of until a year ago, and now will never forget, there hangs a large, white, newly painted board, bearing a notice in black letters six inches high. Exactly underneath the board, rubbing their noses appre-

ciatively against the sign-post, stand two mules,
attached to a limbered waggon, the property of
the A.S.C. Their charioteers are sitting adjacent,
in a convenient shell-hole, partaking of luncheon.

"That was a rotten place we 'ad to wait in
yesterday, Sammy," observes Number One. "The
draught was somethink cruel."

The recumbent Samuel agrees. "This little
'oller is a bit of all right," he remarks. "When
you 've done strarfin' that bully-beef, 'and it
over, ole man!"

He leans his head back upon the lip of the shell-
hole, and gazes pensively at the notice-board six
feet away. It says: —

> # VERY DANGEROUS.
> # DO NOT
> # LOITER
> # HERE.

III

Here is another cross-roads, a good mile farther
forward — and less than a hundred yards behind
the fire-trench. It is dawn.

The roads themselves are not so distinct as they
were. They are becoming grass-grown: for more
than a year — in daylight at least — no human
foot has trodden them. The place is like hundreds

of others that you may see scattered up and down this countryside — two straight, flat, metalled country roads, running north and south and east and west, crossing one another at a faultless right angle.

Of the four corners thus created, one is — or was — occupied by an estaminet: you can still see the sign, *Estaminet au Commerce*, over the door. Two others contain cottages, — the remains of cottages. At the fourth, facing south and east, stands what is locally known as a "Calvaire," — a bank of stone, a lofty cross, and a life-size figure of Christ, facing east, towards the German lines.

This spot is shelled every day — has been shelled every day for months. Possibly the enemy suspects a machine-gun or an observation post amid the tumble-down buildings. Hardly one brick remains upon another. And yet — the sorrowful Figure is unbroken. The Body is riddled with bullets — in the glowing dawn you may count not five but fifty wounds — but the Face is untouched. It is the standing miracle of this most materialistic war. Throughout the length of France you will see the same thing.

Agnostics ought to come out here, for a "cure."

IV

With spring comes also the thought of the Next Push.

But we do not talk quite so glibly of pushes as we did. Neither, for that matter, does Brother Boche. He has just completed six weeks' pushing at Verdun, and is beginning to be a little uncer-

tain as to which direction the pushing is coming
from.

No; once more the military textbooks are being rewritten. We started this war under one
or two rather fallacious premises. One was that
Artillery was more noisy than dangerous. When
Antwerp fell, we rescinded that theory. Then the
Boche set out to demonstrate that an Attack,
provided your Artillery preparation is sufficiently
thorough, and you are prepared to set *no* limit to
your expenditure of Infantry, must ultimately
succeed. To do him justice, the Boche supported
his assertions very plausibly. His phalanx bundled the Russians all the way from Tannenburg to
Riga. The Austrians adopted similar tactics, with
similar results.

We were duly impressed. The world last summer did not quite realize how far the results of
the campaign were due to German efficiency and
how far to Russian unpreparedness. (Russia, we
realise now, found herself in the position of the
historic Mrs. Partington, who endeavoured to
repel the Atlantic with a mop. This year, we
understand, she is [in a position to discard the
mop in favour of something far, far better.)

Then came — Verdun. Military science turned
over yet another page, and noted that against
consummate generalship, unlimited munitions,
and selfless devotion on the part of the defence,
the most spectacular and highly-doped phalanx
can spend itself in vain. Military science also
noted that, under modern conditions, the capture
of this position or that signifies nothing: the only

method of computing victory is to count the dead
on either side. On that reckoning, the French at
Verdun have already gained one of the great vic-
tories of all time.

"In fact," said Colonel Kemp, "this war will
end when the Boche has lost so many men as to
be unable to man his present trench-line, and not
before."

"You don't think, sir, that we shall make another Push?" suggested Angus M'Lachlan eagerly. The others were silent: they had experienced a Push already.

"Not so long as the Boche continues to play
our game for us, by attacking. If he tumbles to
the error he is making, and digs himself in again
— well, it may become necessary to draw him.
In that case, M'Lachlan, you shall have first chop
at the Victoria Crosses. Afraid I can't recom-
mend you for your last exploit, though I admit it
must have required some nerve!"

There was unseemly laughter at this allusion.
Four nights previously Angus had been sent out
in charge of a wiring-party. He had duly crawled
forth with his satellites, under cover of darkness,
on to No Man's Land; and, there selecting a row
of "knife-rests" which struck him as being badly
in need of repair, had well and truly reinforced
the same with many strands of the most barbar-
ous brand of barbed wire. This, despite more
than usually fractious behaviour upon the part
of the Boche.

Next morning, through a sniper's loophole, he
exhibited the result of his labours to Major Wag-

staffe. The Major gazed long and silently upon
his subordinate's handiwork. There was no mistaking it. It stood out bright and gleaming in the
rays of the rising sun, amid its dingy surroundings
of rusty ironmongery. Angus M'Lachlan waited
anxiously for a little praise.

"Jolly good piece of work," said Major Wagstaffe at last. "But tell me, why have you re-
paired the Boche wire instead of your own?"

"The only enemy we have to fear," continued
Colonel Kemp, rubbing his spectacles savagely,
"is the free and independent British voter — I
mean, the variety of the species that we have left
at home. Like the gentleman in Jack Point's
song, 'He likes to get value for money'; and he is
quite capable of asking us, about June or July,
'if we know that we are paid to be funny?' —
before we are ready. What's your view of the
situation at home, Wagstaffe? You're the last
off leave."

Wagstaffe shook his head.

"The British Nation," he said, "is quite mad.
That fact, of course, has been common property
on the Continent of Europe ever since Cook's
Tours were invented. But what irritates the orderly Boche is that there is no method in its mad-
ness. Nothing you can go upon, or take hold of, or
wring any advantage from."

"As how?"

"Well, take compulsory service. For genera-
tions the electorate of our country has been
trained by a certain breed of politician — the

Bandar-log of the British Constitution — to howl
down such a low and degrading business as
National Defence. A nasty Continental custom,
they called it. Then came the War, and the glorious Voluntary System got to work."

"Aided," the Colonel interpolated, "by a campaign of mural advertisement which a cinema
star's press agent would have boggled at!"

"Quite so," agreed Wagstaffe. "Next, when
the Voluntary System had done its damnedest —
in other words, when the willing horse had been
worked to his last ounce — we tried the Derby
Scheme. The manhood of the nation was divided
into groups, and a fresh method of touting for
troops was adopted. Married shysters, knowing
that at least twenty groups stood between them
and a job of work, attested in comparatively large
numbers. The single shysters were less reckless
— so much less reckless, in fact, that compulsion
began to materialise at last."

"But only for single shysters," said Bobby
Little regretfully.

"Yes; and the married shyster rejoiced accordingly. But the single shyster is a most subtle rep-
tile. On examination, it was found that the single members of this noble army of martyrs were
all 'starred,' or 'reserved', or 'ear-marked' — or
whatever it is that they do to these careful fellows.
So the poor old married shyster, who had only
attested to show his blooming patriotism and
encourage the others, suddenly found himself
confronted with the awful prospect of having to
defend his country personally, instead of by let-

ter to the halfpenny press. Then the fat was fairly
in the fire! The married martyr —"

"Come, come, old man! Not all of them!"
said Colonel Kemp. "I have a married brother of
my own, a solicitor of thirty-eight, who is simply
clamouring for active service!"

"I know that, sir," admitted Wagstaffe quickly.
"Thank God, these fellows are only a minority,
and a freak minority at that; but freak minorities
seem to get the monopoly of the limelight in our
unhappy country."

"The whole affair," mused the Colonel, "can
hardly be described as a frenzied rally round the
Old Flag. By God," he broke out suddenly, "it
fairly makes one's blood boil! When I think of the
countless good fellows, married and single, but
mainly married, who left *all* and followed the call
of common decency and duty the moment the
War broke out — most of them now dead or crip-
pled; and when I see this miserable handful of
shirkers, holding up vital public business while
the pros and cons of their wretched claims to
exemption are considered — well, I almost wish I
had been born a Boche!"

"I don't think you need apply for naturalisa-
tion papers yet, Colonel," said Wagstaffe. "The
country is perfectly sound at heart over this question, and always was. The present agitation, as I
say, is being engineered by the more verminous
section of our incomparable daily Press, for its
own ends. It makes our Allies lift their eyebrows
a bit; but they are sensible people, and they realise that although we are a nation of lunatics,

we usually deliver the goods in the end. As for
the Boche, poor fellow, the whole business makes
him perfectly rabid. Here he is, with all his
splendid organisation and brutal efficiency, and
he can't even knock a dent into our undisci-
plined, back-chatting, fool-ridden, self-depreciat-
ing old country! I, for one, sympathise with the
Boche profoundly. On paper, we don't *deserve* to
win!"

"But we shall!" remarked that single-minded
paladin, Bobby Little.

"Of course we shall! And what's more, we are
going to derive a national benefit out of this war
which will in itself be worth the price of admis-
sion!"

"How?" asked several voices.

Wagstaffe looked round the table. The Battalion were for the moment in Divisional Reserve,
and consequently out of the trenches. Some one
had received a box of Coronas from home, and
the mess president had achieved a bottle of port.
Hence the present symposium at Headquarters
Mess. Wagstaffe's eyes twinkled.

"Will each officer present," he said, "kindly
name his pet aversion among his fellow-crea-
tures?"

"A person or a type?" asked Mr. Waddell cautiously.

"A type."

Colonel Kemp led off.

"Male ballet-dancers," he said.

"Fat, shiny men," said Bobby Little, "with
walrus mustaches!"

"All conscientious objectors, passive resisters, pacifists, and other cranks!" continued the orthodox Waddell.

"All people who go on strike during war-time," said the Adjutant. There was an approving murmur — then silence.

"Your contribution, M'Lachlan?" said Wagstaffe.

Angus, who had kept silence from shyness, suddenly blazed out: —

"I think," he said, "that the most contemptible people in the world to-day are those politicians and others who, in years gone by, systematically cried down anything in the shape of national defence or national inclination to personal service, because they saw there were no *votes* in such a programme; and who *now*" — Angus's passion rose to fever-heat, — "stand up and endeavour to cultivate popular favour by reviling the Ministry and the Army for want of preparedness and initiative. Such men do not deserve to live! Oh, sirs —"

But Angus's peroration was lost in a storm of applause.

"You are adjudged to have hit the bull's-eye, M'Lachlan," said Colonel Kemp. "But tell us, Wagstaffe, your exact object in compiling this horrible catalogue."

"Certainly. It is this. Universal Service is a *fait accompli* at last, or is shortly going to be — and without anything very much in the way of exemption either. When it comes, just think of it! All these delightful people whom we have been

enumerating will have to toe the line at last. For
the first time in their little lives they will learn the
meaning of discipline, and fresh air, and *ésprit de
corps.* Is n't that worth a war? If the present
scrap can only be prolonged for another year, our
country will receive a tonic which will carry it on
for another century. Think of it! Great Britain,
populated by men who have actually been outside
their own parish; men who know that the whole
is greater than the part; men who are too wide
awake to go on doing just what the *Bandar-log* tell
them, and allow themselves to be used as stalking-
horses for low-down political ramps! When *we,*
going round in bath-chairs and on crutches, see
that sight — well, I don't think we shall regret
our missing arms and legs quite so much, Colonel. War is Hell, and all that; but there is one
worse thing than a long war, and that is a long
peace!"

"I wonder!" said Colonel Kemp reflectively.
He was thinking of his wife and four children in
distant Argyllshire.

But the rapt attitude and quickened breath of
Temporary Captain BobbyLittle endorsed every
word that Major Wagstaffe had spoken. As he
rolled into his "flea-bag" that night, Bobby re-
quoted to himself, for the hundredth time, a passage from Shakespeare which had recently come
to his notice. He was not a Shakespearian scholar,
nor indeed a student of literature at all; but these
lines had been sent to him, cut out of a daily
almanac, by an equally unlettered and very ador-
able confidante at home: —

"And gentlemen in England now a-bed,
  Shall think themselves accursed they were not here,
  And hold their manhoods cheap whiles any speaks
  That fought with us upon Saint Crispin's day!"

Bobby was the sort of person who would thoroughly have enjoyed the Battle of Agincourt.

VIIl

I

WE will call the village St. Grégoire. That is not
its real name; because the one thing you must not
do in war-time is to call a thing by its real name.
To take a hackneyed example, you do not call
a spade a spade: you refer to it, officially, as
Shovels, General Service, One. This helps to de-
ceive, and ultimately to surprise, the enemy; and
as we all know by this time, surprise is the essence
of successful warfare. On the same principle, if
your troops are forced back from their front-line
trenches, you call this "successfully straightening
out an awkward salient."

But this by the way. Let us get back to
St. Grégoire. Hither, mud-splashed, ragged, hol-
low-cheeked, came our battalion — they call us
the Seventh Hairy Jocks nowadays — after four
months' continuous employment in the firing-line.
Ypres was a household word to them; Plugstreet
was familiar ground; Givenchy they knew inti-
mately; Loos was their wash-pot — or rather, a
collection of wash-pots, for in winter all the shell-
craters are full to overflowing. In addition to their
prolonged and strenuous labours in the trenches,
the Hairy Jocks had taken part in a Push — a
part not altogether unattended with glory, but
prolific in casualties. They had not been "pulled

out" to rest and refit for over six months, for
Divisions on the Western Front were not at
that period too numerous, the voluntary system
being at its last gasp, while the legions of Lord
Derby had not yet crystallised out of the ocean of
public talk which held them in solution. So the
Seventh Hairy Jocks were bone tired. But they
were as hard as a rigorous winter in the open
could make them, and — they were going back to
rest at last. Had not their beloved C.O. told them
so? And he had added, in a voice not altogether
free from emotion, that if ever men deserved a
solid rest and a good time, "you boys do!"

So the Hairy Jocks trudged along the long,
straight, nubbly French road, well content, spec-
ulating with comfortable pessimism as to the
character of the billets in which they would find
themselves.

Meanwhile, ten miles ahead, the advance party
were going round the town in quest of the billets.

Billet-hunting on the Western Front is not
quite so desperate an affair as hunting for lodgings
at Margate, because in the last extremity you can
always compel the inhabitants to take you in —
or at least, exert pressure to that end through the
Mairie. But at the best one's course is strewn
with obstacles, and fortunate is the Adjutant who
has to his hand a subaltern capable of finding
lodgings for a thousand men without making a
mess of it.

The billeting officer on this, as on most occasions, was our friend Cockerell, — affectionately
known to the entire Battalion as "Sparrow," —

and his qualifications for the post were derived
from three well-marked and invaluable characteristics, namely, an imperious disposition, a thick
skin, and an attractive *bonhomie* of manner.

Behold him this morning dismounting from his
horse in the *place* of St. Grégoire. Around him are
grouped his satellites — the Quartermaster-Sergeant, four Company Sergeants, some odd orderlies, and a forlorn little man in a neat drab uniform with light blue facings, — the regimental
interpreter. The party have descended, with the
delicate care of those who essay to perform acro-
batic feats in kilts, from bicycles — serviceable
but appallingly heavy machines of Government
manufacture, the property of the "Buzzers," but
commandeered for the occasion. The Quartermaster-Sergeant, who is not accustomed to strenuous exercise, mops his brow and glances expect-
antly round the *place*. His eye comes gently to
rest upon a small but hospitable-looking *estaminet*.

Lieutenant Cockerell examines his wrist-watch.

"Half-past ten!" he announces. "Quartermaster-Sergeant!"

"Sirr!" The Quartermaster-Sergeant unglues
his longing gaze from the *estaminet* and comes
woodenly to attention.

"I am going to see the Town Major about a
billeting area. I will meet you and the party here
in twenty minutes."

Master Cockerell trots off on his mud-splashed
steed, followed by the respectful and appreciative salutes of his followers — appreciative, because a less considerate officer would have taken

the whole party direct to the Town Major's office
and kept them standing in the street, wasting
moments which might have been better employed
elsewhere, until it was time to proceed with the
morning's work.

"How strong are you?" inquired the Town
Major.

Cockerell told him. The Town Major whistled.

"That all? Been doing some job of work,
have n't you?"

Cockerell nodded, and the Town Major proceeded to examine a large-scale plan of St. Grégoire, divided up into different-coloured plots.

"We are rather full up at present," he said;
"but the Cemetery Area is vacant. The Seven-
teenth Geordies moved out yesterday. You can
have that." He indicated a triangular section
with his pencil.

Master Cockerell gave a deprecatory cough.

"We have come here, sir," he intimated dryly,
"for a change of scene."

The stout Town Major — all Town Majors are
stout — chuckled.

"Not bad for a Scot!" he conceded. "But it's
quite a cheery district, really. You won't have
to doss down in the cemetery itself, you know.
These two streets here —" he flicked a pencil —
"will hold practically all your battalion, at its
present strength. There's a capital house in the
Rue Jean Jacques Rousseau which will do for
Battalion Headquarters. The corporal over there
will give you your *billets de logement.*"

"Are there any other troops in the area, sir?" asked Cockerell, who, as already indicated, was no child in these matters.

"There ought not to be, of course. But you know what the Heavy Gunners and the A.S.C. are! If you come across any of them, fire them out. If they wear too many stars and crowns for you, let me know, and I will perform the feat myself. You fellows need a good rest and no worries, I know. Good-morning."

At ten minutes to eleven Cockerell found the Quartermaster-Sergeant and party, wiping their mustaches and visibly refreshed, at the exact spot where he had left them; and the hunt for billets began.

"A" Company were easily provided for, a derelict tobacco factory being encountered at the head of the first street. Lieutenant Cockerell accordingly detached a sergeant and a corporal from his train, and passed on. The wants of "B" Company were supplied by commandeering a block of four dilapidated houses farther down the street — all in comparatively good repair except the end house, whose roof had been disarranged by a shell during the open fighting in the early days of the war.

This exhausted the possibilities of the first street, and the party debouched into the second, which was long and straggling, and composed entirely of small houses.

"Now for a bit of the retail business!" said Master Cockerell resignedly. "Sergeant M'Nab, what is the strength of 'C' Company?"

"One hunner and thairty-fower other ranks, sirr," announced Sergeant M'Nab, consulting a much-thumbed roll-book.

"We shall have to put them in twos and threes all down the street," said Cockerell. "Come on; the longer we look at it the less we shall like it. Interpreter!"

The forlorn little man, already described, trotted up, and saluted with open hand, French fashion. His name was Baptiste Bombominet ("or words to that effect," as the Adjutant put it), and may have been so inscribed upon the regimental roll; but throughout the rank and file Baptiste was affectionately known by the generic title of "Alphonso." The previous seven years had been spent by him in the congenial and blameless atmosphere of a Ladies' Tailor's in the west end of London, where he enjoyed the status and emoluments of chief cutter. Now, called back to his native land by the voice of patriotic obligation, he found himself selected, by virtue of a residence of seven years in England, to act as official interpreter between a Scottish Regiment which could not speak English, and Flemish peasants who could not speak French. No wonder that his pathetic brown eyes always appeared full of tears. However, he followed Cockerell down the street, and meekly embarked upon a contest with the lady inhabitants thereof, in which he was hopelessly outmatched from the start.

At the first door a dame of massive proportions, but keen business instincts, announced her total inability to accommodate *soldats*, but explained that she would be pleased to entertain *officiers* to any number. This is a common gambit. Twenty British privates in your *grenier*, though extraordinarily well-behaved as a class, make a good deal of noise, buy little, and leave mud everywhere. On the other hand, two or three officers give no trouble, and can be relied upon to consume and pay for unlimited omelettes and bowls of coffee.

That seasoned vessel, Lieutenant Cockerell, turned promptly to the Sergeant and Corporal of "C" Company.

"Sergeant M'Nab," he said, "you and Corporal Downie will billet here." He introduced hostess and guests by an expressive wave of the hand. But shrewd Madame was not to be bluffed.

"*Pas de sergents, Monsieur le Capitaine!*" she exclaimed. "*Officiers!*"

"*Ils sont officiers — sous-officiers,*" explained Cockerell, rather ingeniously, and moved off down the street.

At the next house the owner — a small, wizened lady of negligible physique but great staying power — entered upon a duet with Alphonso, which soon reduced that very moderate performer to breathlessness. He shrugged his shoulders feebly,. and cast an appealing glance towards the Lieutenant.

"What does she say?" inquired Cockerell.

"She say dis 'ouse no good, sair! She 'ave seven children, and one *malade* — seek."

"Let me see," commanded the practical officer.

He insinuated himself as politely as possible past his reluctant opponent, and walked down the

narrow passage into the kitchen. Here he turned,
and inquired —

"Er — *où est la pauvre petite chose?*"

Madame promptly opened a door, and displayed a little girl in bed — a very flushed and
feverish little girl.

Cockerell grinned sympathetically at the patient, to that young lady's obvious gratification;
and turned to the mother.

"*Je suis très — triste,*" he said; "*j'ai grand mis-
éricorde. Je ne placerai pas de soldats ici. Bon
jour!*"

By this time he was in the street again. He
saluted politely and departed, followed by the
grateful regards of Madame.

No special difficulties were encountered at the
next few houses. The ladies at the house-door
were all polite; many of them were most friendly;
but naturally each was anxious to get as few men
and as many officers as possible — except the
proprietess of an *estaminet*, who offered to accommodate the entire regiment. However, with a little tact here and a little firmness there, Master
Cockerell succeeded in distributing "C" Company among some dozen houses. One old gentleman, with a black alpaca cap and a six-days
beard, proprietor of a lofty establishment at the
corner of the street, proved not only recalcitrant,
but abusive. With him Cockerell dealt promptly.

"*Ça suffit!*" he announced. "*Montrez-moi votre grenier!*"

The old man, grumbling, led the way up numerous rickety staircases to the inevitable loft

under the tiles. This proved to be a noble apartment thirty feet long. From wall to wall stretched innumerable strings.

"We can get a whole platoon in here," said Cockerell contentedly. "Tell him, Alphonso. These people," he explained to Sergeant M'Nab, "always dislike giving up their lofts, because they hang their laundry there in winter. However, the old boy must lump it. After all, we are in this country for his health, not ours; and he gets paid for every man who sleeps here. That fixes 'C' Company. Now for 'D'! The other side of the street this time."

Quarters were found in due course for "D" Company; after which Cockerell discovered a vacant building-site which would serve for transport lines. An empty garage was marked down for the Quartermaster's ration store, and the Quartermaster-Sergeant promptly faded into its recesses with a grateful sigh. An empty shop in the Rue Jean Jacques Rousseau, conveniently adjacent to Battalion Headquarters, was appropriated for that gregarious band, the regimental signallers and telephone section; while a suitable home for the Anarchists, or Bombers, together with their stock-in-trade, was found in the basement of a remote dwelling on the outskirts of the area.

After this, Lieutenant Cockerell, left alone with Alphonso and the orderly in charge of his horse, heaved a sigh of exhaustion and transferred his attention from his notebook to his watch.

"That finishes the rank and file," he said. "I

breakfasted at four this morning, and the battalion won't arrive for a couple of hours yet. Alphonso, I am going to have an omelette somewhere. I shall want you in half an hour exactly. Don't go wandering off for the rest of the day, pinching soft billets for yourself and the Sergeant-Major and your other pals, as you usually do!"

Alphonso saluted guiltily — evidently the astute Cockerell had "touched the spot" — and was turning away, when suddenly the billeting officer's eye encountered an illegible scrawl at the very foot of his list.

"Stop a moment, Alphonso! I have forgotten those condemned machine-gunners, as usual. *Strafe* them! Come on! Once more into the breach, Alphonso! There is a little side-alley down here that we have not tried."

The indefatigable Cockerell turned down the Rue Gambetta, followed by Alphonso, faint but resigned.

"Here is the very place!" announced Cockerell almost at once. "This house, Number Five. We can put the gunners and their little guns into that stable at the back, and the officer can have a room in the house itself. *Sonnez*, for the last time before lunch!"

The door was opened by a pleasant-faced young woman of about thirty, who greeted Cockerell—tartan is always popular with French ladies — with a beaming smile, but shook her head regretfully upon seeing the *billet de logement* in his hand. The inevitable duet with Alphonso followed. Presently Alphonso turned to his superior.

"Madame is ver' sorry, sair, but an *officier* is here already."

"Show me the *officier!*" replied the prosaic Cockerell.

The duet was resumed.

"Madame say," announced Alphonso presently, "that the *officier* is not here now; but he will return."

"So will Christmas! Meanwhile I am going to put an *Emma Gee* officer in here."

Alphonso's desperate attempt to translate the foregoing idiom into French was interrupted by Madame's retirement into the house, whither she beckoned Cockerell to follow her. In the front room she produced a frayed sheet of paper, which she proffered with an apologetic smile. The paper said: —

This billet is entirely reserved for the Supply Officer of this District. It is not to be occupied by troops passing through the town.
                    By Order.

Lieutenant Cockerell whistled softly and vindictively through his teeth.

"Well," he said, "for consummate and concentrated nerve, give me the underlings of the A.S.C.! This pot-bellied blighter not only butts into an area which does n't belong to him, but actually leaves a chit to warn people off the grass even when he is n't here! He has n't signed the document, I observe. That means that he is a newly joined subaltern, trying to get mistaken for a Brass Hat! I 'll fix *him!*"

With great stateliness Lieutenant Cockerell
tore the offending screed into four portions, to the
audible concern of Madame. But the Lieutenant
smiled reassuringly upon her.

"*Je vous donnerai un autre, vous savez,*" he
assured her.

He sat down at the table, tore a leaf from his
Field Service Pocket Book, and wrote: —

*The Supply Officer of the District is at liberty to
occupy this billet only at such times as it is not required by the troops of the Combatant Services.*
Signed, F. J. Cockerell,
Lieut. & Asst. Adj.,
7th B. & W. Highes.

"That's a pretty nasty one!" he observed with
relish. Then, having pinned the insulting document conspicuously to the mantelpiece, he observed to the mystified lady of the house: —

"*Voilà, Madame. Si l'officier reviendra, je le
verrai moi-même, avec grand plaisir. Bon jour!*"

And with this dark saying Sparrow Cockerell
took his departure.

II

The Battalion, headed by their tatterdemalion
pipers, stumped into the town in due course, and
were met on the outskirts by the billeting party,
who led the various companies to their appointed
place. After inspecting their new quarters, and
announcing with gloomy satisfaction that they
were the worst, dirtiest, and most uncomfortable
yet encountered, everybody settled down in the

best place he could find, and proceeded to make
himself remarkably snug.

Battalion Headquarters and the officers of "A"
Company were billeted in an imposing mansion
which actually boasted a bathroom. It is true
that there was no water, but this deficiency was
soon made good by a string of officers' servants
bearing buckets. Beginning with Colonel Kemp,
who was preceded by an orderly bearing a small
towel and a large loofah, each officer performed a
ceremonial ablution; and it was a collection of
what Major Wagstaffe termed "bright and bonny
young faces" which collected round the Mess table at seven o'clock.

It was in every sense a gala meal. Firstly, it
was weeks since any one (except Second Lieutenant M'Corquodale, newly joined, and addressed,
for painfully obvious reasons, as "Tich") had
found himself at table in an apartment where it
was possible to stand upright. Secondly, the Mess
President had coaxed glass tumblers out of the
ancient *concierge;* and only those who have drunk
from enamelled ironware for weeks on end can
appreciate the pure joy of escape from the in-
determinate metallic flavour which such vessels
impart to all beverages. Thirdly, these same
tumblers were filled to the brim with inferior
but exhilarating champagne — purchased, as they
euphemistically put it in the Supply Column,
"locally." Lastly, the battalion had several
months of hard fighting behind it, probably a full
month's rest before it, and the conscience of duty
done and recognition earned floating like a halo

above it. For the moment memories of Nightmare Wood and the Kidney Bean Redoubt — more especially the latter — were effaced. Even the sorrowful gaps in the ring round the table seemed less noticeable.

The menu, too, was almost pretentious. First came the *hors d'œuvres* — a tin of sardines. This was followed by what the Mess Corporal described as a savoury omelette, but which the Second-in-Command condemned as "a regrettable incident."

"It is false economy," he observed dryly to the Mess President, "to employ Mark One [1] eggs as anything but hand-grenades."

However, the tide of popular favour turned with the haggis, contributed by Lieutenant Angus M'Lachlan, from a parcel from home. Even the fact that the Mess cook, an inexperienced æsthete from Islington, had endeavoured to tone down the naked repulsiveness of the dainty with discreet festoons of tinned macaroni, failed to arouse the resentment of a purely Scottish Mess. The next course — the beef ration, hacked into the inevitable gobbets and thinly disguised by a sprinkling of curry powder — aroused no enthusiasm; but the unexpected production of a large tin of Devonshire cream, contributed by Captain Bobby Little, relieved the canned peaches of their customary monotony. Last of all came a savoury — usually described as *the* savoury — consisting of a raft of toast per person, each raft carrying an

---

[1] In the British army each issue of arms or equipment receives a distinctive "Mark." Mark 1 denotes the earliest issue.

abundant cargo of fried potted meat, and provided with a passenger in the shape of a recumbent sausage.

A compound of grounds and dish-water, described by the optimistic Mess Corporal as coffee, next made its appearance, mitigated by a bottle of Cointreau and a box of Panatellas; and the Mess turned itself to more intellectual refreshment. A heavy and long-overdue mail had been found waiting at St. Grégoire. Letters had been devoured long ago. Now, each member of the Mess leaned back in his chair, straightened his weary legs under the table, and settled down, cigar in mouth, to the perusal of the *Spectator* or the *Tatler*, according to rank and literary taste.

Colonel Kemp, unfolding a week-old *Times*, looked over his glasses at his torpid disciples.

"Where is young Sandeman?" he inquired.

Young Sandeman was the Adjutant.

"He went out to the Orderly Room, sir, five minutes ago," replied Bobby Little.

"I only want to give him to-morrow's Orders. No doubt he'll be back presently. I may as well mention to you fellows that I propose to allow the men three clear days' rest, except for bathing and re-clothing. After that we must do Company Drill, good and hard, so as to polish up the new draft, who are due to-morrow. I am going to start a bombing-school, too: at least seventy-five per cent of the Battalion ought to pass the test before we go back to the line. However, we need not rush things. We should be here in peace for at least a month. We must get up some sports, and

I think it would be a sound scheme to have a sing-song one Saturday night. I was just saying, Sandeman," — this to the Adjutant, who reëntered the room at that moment, — "that it would be a sound —"

The Adjutant laid a pink field-telegraph slip before his superior.

"This has just come in from Brigade Headquarters, sir," he said. "I have sent for the Sergeant-Major."

The Colonel adjusted his glasses and read the despatch. A deathly, sickening silence reigned in the room. Then he looked up.

"I am afraid I was a bit previous," he said quietly. "The Royal Stickybacks have lost the Kidney Bean, and we are detailed to go up and retake it. Great compliment to the regiment, but a trifle mistimed! You young fellows had better go to bed. Parade at 4 A.M., sharp! Good-night! Come along to the Orderly Room, Sandeman."

The door closed, and the Mess, grinding the ends of their cigars into their coffee-cups, heaved themselves resignedly to their aching feet.

"There ain't," quoted Major Wagstaffe, "no word in the blooming language for it!"

III

The Kidney Bean Redoubt is the key to a very considerable sector of trenches.

It lies just behind a low ridge. The two horns of the bean are drawn back out of sight of the enemy, but the middle swells forward over the sky-line and commands an extensive view of the country beyond. Direct observation of artillery fire is possible: consequently an armoured observation post has been constructed here, from which gunner officers can direct the fire of their batteries with accuracy and elegance. Lose the Kidney Bean, and the boot is on the other leg. The enemy has the upper ground now: he can bring observed artillery fire to bear upon all our tenderest spots behind the line. He can also enfilade our front-line trenches.

Well, as already stated, the Twenty-Second Royal Stickybacks had lost the Kidney Bean. They were a battalion of recent formation, stout-hearted fellows all, but new to the refinements of intensive trench warfare. When they took over the sector, they proceeded to leave undone various vital things which the Hairy Jocks had always made a point of doing, and to do various unnecessary things which the Hairy Jocks had never done. The observant Hun promptly recognised that he was faced by a fresh batch of opponents, and, having carefully studied the characteristics of the newcomers, prescribed and administered an exemplary dose of frightfulness. He began by tickling up the Stickybacks with an unpleasant engine called the *Minenwerfer*, which despatches a large sausage-shaped projectile in a series of ridiculous somersaults, high over No Man's Land into the enemy's front-line trench, where it explodes and annihilates everything in that particular bay. Upon these occasions one's only chance of salvation is to make a rapid calculation as to the bay into which the sausage is going

to fall, and then double speedily round a traverse
— or, if possible, two traverses — into another.
It is an exhilarating pastime, but presents complications when played by a large number of persons in a restricted space, especially when the
persons aforesaid are not unanimous as to the
ultimate landing-place of the projectile.

After a day and a night of these aerial torpedoes
the Hun proceeded to an intensive artillery bombardment. He had long coveted the Kidney
Bean, and instinct told him that he would never
have a better opportunity of capturing it than
now. Accordingly, two hours before dawn, the Redoubt was subjected to a sudden, simultaneous,
and converging fire from all the German artillery
for many miles round, the whole being topped
up with a rain of those crowning instruments of
demoralisation, gas-shells. At the same time an
elaborate curtain of shrapnel and high explosive
was let down behind the Redoubt, to serve the
double purpose of preventing either the sending
up of reinforcements or the temporary withdrawal
of the garrison.

At the first streak of dawn the bombardment
was switched off, as if by a tap; the curtain fire
was redoubled in volume; and a massed attack
swept across the disintegrated wire into the shattered and pulverised Redoubt. Other attacks
were launched on either flank; but these were obvious blinds, intended to prevent a too concentrated defence of the Kidney Bean. The Royal
Stickybacks — what was left of them — put up a
tough fight; but half of them were lying dead or

buried, or both, before the assault was launched, and the rest were too dazed and stupefied by noise and chlorine gas to withstand — much less to repel — the overwhelming phalanx that was hurled against them. One by one they went down, until the enemy troops, having swamped the Redoubt, gathered themselves up in a fresh wave and surged towards the reserve-line trenches, four hundred yards distant. At this point, however, they met a strong counter-attack, launched from the Brigade Reserve, and after heavy fighting were bundled back into the Redoubt itself. Here the German machine-guns had staked out a defensive line, and the German retirement came to a standstill.

Meanwhile a German digging party, many hundred strong, had been working madly in No Man's Land, striving to link up the newly acquired ground with the German lines. By the afternoon the Kidney Bean was not only "reversed and consolidated," but was actually included in the enemy's front trench system. Altogether a well-planned and admirably executed little operation.

Forty-eight hours later the Kidney Bean Redoubt was recaptured, and remains in British hands to this day. Many arms of the Service took honourable part in the enterprise — heavy guns, field guns, trench-mortars, machine-guns; Sappers and Pioneers; Infantry in various capacities. But this narrative is concerned only with the part played by the Seventh Hairy Jocks.

"Sorry to pull you back from rest, Colonel,"

said the Brigadier, when the commander of the
Hairy Jocks reported; "but the Divisional General considers that the only feasible way to hunt
the Boche from the Kidney Bean is to bomb him
out of it. That means trench-fighting, pure and
simple. I have called you up because you fellows
know the ins and outs of the Kidney Bean as no
one else does. The Brigade who are in the line
just now are quite new to the place. Here is an
aeroplane photograph of the Redoubt, as at present constituted. Tell off your own bombing parties; make your own dispositions; send me a copy
of your provisional orders; and I will fit my plan
in with yours. The Corps Commander has promised to back you with every gun, trench-mortar,
culverin, and arquebus in his possession."

In due course Battalion Orders were issued and
approved. They dealt with operations most bar-
barous amid localities of the most homelike sound.
Number Nine Platoon, for instance (Commander
Lieutenant Cockerell), were to proceed in single
file, carrying so many grenades per man, up Char-
ing Cross Road, until stopped by the barrier
which the enemy were understood to have erected
in Trafalgar Square, where a bombing-post and at
least one machine-gun would probably be encountered. At this point they were to wait until Trafalgar Square had been suitably dealt with by a
trench-mortar. (Here followed a paragraph addressed exclusively to the Trench-Mortar Officer.)
After this the bombers of Number Three Platoon
would bomb their way across the Square and up
the Strand. Another party would clear North-

umberland Avenue, while a Lewis gun raked
Whitehall. And so on. Every detail was thought
out, down to the composition of the parties which
were to "clean up" afterwards — that is, extract
the reluctant Boche from various underground
fastnesses well known to the extractors. The whole
enterprise was then thoroughly rehearsed in some
dummy trenches behind the line, until every one
knew his exact part. Such is modern warfare.

Next day the Kidney Bean Redoubt was in
British hands again. The Hun — what was left
of him after an intensive bombardment of twenty-
four hours — had betaken himself back over the
ridge, *via* the remnants of his two new communication trenches, to his original front line. The
two communication trenches themselves were
blocked and sandbagged, and were being heavily
supervised by a pair of British machine-guns.
Fighting in the Redoubt itself had almost ceased,
though a humorous sergeant, followed by acolytes
bearing bombs, was still "combing out" certain
residential districts in the centre of the maze.
Ever and anon he would stoop down at the entrance of some deep dug-out, and bawl —

"Ony mair doon there? Come away, Fritz!
I'll gie ye five seconds. Yin, Twa, Three —"

Then, with a rush like a bolt of rabbits, two or
three close-cropped, grimy Huns would scuttle up
from below and project themselves from one of
the exits; to be taken in charge by grinning Cale-
donians wearing "tin hats" very much awry, and
escorted back through the barrage to the "prisoners' base" in rear.

All through the day, amidst unremitting shell
fire and local counter-attack, the Hairy Jocks re-
consolidated the Kidney Bean; and they were
so far successful that when they handed over the
work to another battalion at dusk, the parapet
was restored, the machine-guns were in position,
and a number of "knife-rest" barbed-wire en-
tanglements were lying just behind the trench,
ready to be hoisted over the parapet and joined
together in a continuous defensive line as soon as
the night was sufficiently dark.

One by one the members of Number Nine
Platoon squelched — for it had rained hard all
day — back to the reserve line. They were utterly exhausted, and still inclined to feel a little
aggrieved at having been pulled out from rest;
but they were well content. They had done the
State some service, and they knew it; and they
knew that the higher powers knew it too. There
would be some very flattering reading in Divisional Orders in a few days' time.

Meanwhile, their most pressing need was for
something to eat. To be sure, every man had
gone into action that morning carrying his day's
rations. But the British soldier, improvident as
the grasshopper, carries his day's rations in one
place, and one place only — his stomach. The
Hairy Jocks had eaten what they required at their
extremely early breakfast: the residue thereof
they had abandoned.

About midnight Master Cockerell, in obedi-
ence to a most welcome order, led the remnants
of his command, faint but triumphant, back from

the reserve line to a road junction two miles in
rear, known as Dead Dog Corner. Here the Battalion was to *rendezvous*, and march back by easy
stages to St. Grégoire. Their task was done.

But at the cross-roads Number Nine Platoon
found no Battalion: only a solitary subaltern,
with his orderly. This young Casabianca informed Cockerell that he, Second Lieutenant
Candlish, had been left behind to "bring in stragglers."

"Stragglers?" exclaimed the infuriated Cockerell. "Do we look like stragglers?"

"No," replied the youthful Candlish frankly;
"you look more like sweeps. However, you had
better push on. The Battalion is n't far ahead.
The order is to march straight back to St. Grégoire and re-occupy former billets."

"What about rations?"

"Rations? The Quartermaster was waiting
here for us when we *rendezvoused*, and every man
had a full ration and a tot of rum." (Number
Nine Platoon cleared their parched throats ex-
pectantly.) "But I fancy he has gone on with the
column. However, if you leg it you should catch
them up. They can't be more than two miles
ahead. So long!"

IV

But the task was hopeless. Number Nine Platoon had been bombing, hacking, and digging all
day. Several of them were slightly wounded —
the serious cases had been taken off long ago by
the stretcher-bearers — and Cockerell's own head

was still dizzy from the fumes of a German gas-
shell.

He lined up his disreputable paladins in the
darkness, and spoke —

"Sergeant M'Nab, how many men are present?"

"Eighteen, sirr." The platoon had gone into
action thirty-four strong.

"How many men are deficient of an emergency
ration? I can make a good guess, but you had
better find out."

Five minutes later the Sergeant reported.
Cockerell's guess was correct. The British private has only one point of view about the
portable property of the State. To him, as an
individual, the sacred emergency ration is an unnecessary encumbrance, and the carrying thereof
a "fatigue." Consequently, when engaged in battle, one of the first (of many) things which he jet-
tisons is this very ration. When all is over, he
reports with unctuous solemnity that the prov-
ender in question has been blown out of his haversack by a shell. The Quartermaster-Sergeant
writes it off as "lost owing to the exigencies of
military service," and indents for another.

Lieutenant Cockerell's haversack contained a
packet of meat-lozenges and about half a pound
of chocolate. These were presented to the Sergeant.

"Hand these round as far as they will go, Sergeant," said Cockerell. "They'll make a mouth-
ful a man, anyhow. Tell the platoon to lie down
for ten minutes; then we'll push off. It's only

fifteen miles. We ought to make it by breakfast-time . . ."

Slowly, mechanically, all through the winter night the victors hobbled along. Cockerell led the way, carrying the rifle of a man with a wounded arm. Occasionally he checked his bearings with map and electric torch. Sergeant M'Nab, who, under a hirsute and attenuated exterior, concealed a constitution of ferro-concrete and the heart of a lion, brought up the rear, uttering fallacious assurances to the faint-hearted as to the shortness of the distance now to be covered, and carrying two rifles.

The customary halts were observed. At ten minutes to four the men flung themselves down for the third time. They had covered about seven miles, and were still eight or nine from St. Grégoire. The everlasting constellation of Verey lights still rose and fell upon the eastern horizon behind them, but the guns were silent.

"There might be a Heavy Battery dug in somewhere about here," mused Cockerell. "I wonder if we could touch them for a few tins of bully. Hallo, what's that?"

A distant rumble came from the north, and out of the darkness loomed a British motor-lorry, lurching and swaying along the rough cobbles of the *pavé*. Some of Cockerell's men were lying dead asleep in the middle of the road, right at the junction. The lorry was going twenty miles an hour.

"Get into the side of the road, you men!" shouted Cockerell, "or they'll run over you. You know what these M.T. drivers are!"

With indignant haste, and at the last possible
moment, the kilted figures scattered to either side
of the narrow causeway. The usual stereotyped
and vitriolic remonstrances were hurled after the
great hooded vehicle as it lurched past.

And then, a most unusual thing happened. The
lorry slowed down, and finally stopped, a hundred yards away. An officer descended, and began
to walk back. Cockerell rose to his weary feet
and walked to meet him.

The officer wore a major's crown upon the
shoulder-straps of his sheepskin-lined "British
Warm" and the badge of the Army Service Corps
upon his cap. Cockerell, indignant at the manner
in which his platoon had been hustled off the
road, saluted stiffly, and muttered: "Good-morning, sir!"

"Good-morning!" said the Major. He was a
stout man of nearly fifty, with twinkling blue
eyes and a short-clipped mustache. Cockerell
judged him to be one of the few remnants of the
original British Army.

"I stopped," explained the older man, "to
apologise for the scandalous way that fellow drove
over you. It was perfectly damnable; but you
know what these converted taxi-drivers are!
This swine forgot for the moment that he had an
officer on board, and hogged it as usual. He goes
under arrest as soon as we get back to billets."

"Thank you very much, sir," said Master
Cockerell, entirely thawed. "I'm afraid my chaps
were lying all over the road; but they are pretty
well down and out at present."

"Where have you come from?" inquired the Major, turning a curious eye upon Cockerell's prostrate followers.

Cockerell explained. When he had finished, he added wistfully —

"I suppose you have not got an odd tin or two of bully to give away, sir? My fellows are about—"

For answer, the Major took the Lieutenant by the arm and led him towards the lorry.

"You have come," he announced, "to the very man you want. I am practically Mr. Harrod. In fact, I am a Corps Supply Officer. How would a Maconochie apiece suit your boys?"

Cockerell, repressing the ecstatic phrases which crowded to his tongue, replied that that was just what the doctor had ordered.

"Where are you bound for?" continued the Major.

"St. Grégoire."

"Of course. You were pulled out from there, were n't you? I am going to St. Grégoire myself as soon as I have finished my round. Home to bed, in fact. I have n't had any sleep worth writing home about for four nights. It is no joke tearing about a country full of shell-holes, hunting for people who have shifted their ration-dump seven times in four days. However, I suppose things will settle down again, now that you fellows have fired Brother Boche out of the Kidney Bean. Pretty fine work, too! Tell me, what is your strength, here and now?"

"One officer," said Cockerell soberly, "and eighteen other ranks."

"All that's left of your platoon?"

Cockerell nodded. The stout Major began to beat upon the tailboard of the lorry with his stick.

"Sergeant Smurthwaite!" he shouted.

There came a muffled grunt from the recesses of the lorry. Then a round and ruddy face rose like a harvest moon above the tailboard, and a stertorous voice replied respectfully —

"Sir?"

"Let down this tailboard; load this officer's platoon into the lorry; issue them with a Maconochie and a tot of rum apiece; and don't forget to put Smee under arrest for dangerous driving when we get back to billets."

"Very good, sir."

Ten minutes later the survivors of Number Nine Platoon, soaked to the skin, dazed, slightly incredulous, but at peace with all the world, reclined close-packed upon the floor of the swaying lorry. Each man held an open tin of Mr. Maconochie's admirable ration between his knees. Perfect silence reigned: a pleasant aroma of rum mellowed the already vitiated atmosphere.

In front, beside the chastened Mr. Smee, sat the Major and Master Cockerell. The latter had just partaken of his share of refreshment, and was now endeavouring, with lifeless fingers, to light a cigarette.

The Major scrutinised his guest intently. Then he stripped off his British Warm coat — incidentally revealing the fact that he wore upon his tunic the ribbons of both South African Medals and

the Distinguished Service Order — and threw it
round Cockerell's shoulders.

"I'm sorry, boy!" he said. "I never noticed.
You are chilled to the bone. Button this round
you."

Cockerell made a feeble protest, but was cut
short.

"Nonsense! There's no sense in taking risks
after you've done your job."

Cockerell assented, a little sleepily. His allow-
ance of rum was bringing its usual vulgar but
comforting influence to bear upon an exhausted
system.

"I see you have been wounded, sir," he observed, noting with a little surprise two gold
stripes upon his host's left sleeve — the sleeve of
a "non-combatant."

"Yes," said the Major. "I got the first one at
Le Cateau. He was only a little fellow; but the
second, which arrived at the Second Show at
Ypres, gave me such a stiff leg that I am only an
old crock now. I was second-in-command of an
Infantry Battalion in those days. In these, I am
only a peripatetic Lipton. However, I am lucky
to be here at all: I've had twenty-seven years'
service. How old are you?"

"Twenty," replied Cockerell. He was too tired
to feel as ashamed as he usually did at having to
confess to the tenderness of his years.

The Major nodded thoughtfully.

"Yes," he said; "I judged that would be about
the figure. My son would have been twenty this
month, only — he was at Neuve Chapelle. He

was very like you in appearance — very. His
mother would have been interested to meet you.
You might as well take a nap for half an hour. I
have two more calls to make, and we shan't get
home till nearly seven. Lean on me, old man.
I'll see you don't tumble overboard . . ."

So Lieutenant Cockerell, conqueror of the
Kidney Bean, fell asleep, his head resting, with
scandalous disregard for military etiquette, upon
the shoulder of the stout Major.

v

An hour or two later, Number Nine Platoon,
distended with concentrated nourishment and
painfully straightening its cramped limbs, de-
canted itself from the lorry into a little *cul-de-
sac* opening off the Rue Jean Jacques Rousseau in
St. Grégoire. The name of the *cul-de-sac* was the
Rue Gambetta.

Their commander, awake and greatly refreshed,
looked round him and realised, with a sudden
sense of uneasiness, that he was in familiar surroundings. The lorry had stopped at the door of
Number Five.

"I don't suppose your Battalion will get back
for some time," said the Major. "Tell your Sergeant to put your men into the stable behind this
house — there's plenty of straw there — and —"

"Their own billet is just round the corner, sir,"
replied Cockerell. "They might as well go there,
thank you."

"Very good. But come in with me yourself,
and doss here for a few hours. You can report to

your C.O. later in the day, when he arrives. This is my *pied-à-terre*," — rapping on the door. "You won't find many billets like it. As you see, it stands in this little backwater, and is not included in any of the regular billeting areas of the town. The Town Major has allotted it to me permanently. Pretty decent of him, was n't it? And Madame Vinot is a dear. Here she is! *Bonjour, Madame Vinot! Avez-vous un feu* — er — *inflammé pour moi dans la chambre ?* " Evidently the Major's French was on a par with Cockerell's.

But Madame understood him, bless her!

"*Mais oui, M'sieur le Colonel!*" she exclaimed cheerfully — the rank of Major is not recognised by the French civilian population — and threw open the door of the sitting-room, with a glance of compassion upon the Major's mud-splashed companion, whom she failed to recognise.

A bright fire was burning in the open stove.

Immediately above, pinned to the mantelpiece and fluttering in the draught, hung Cockerell's manifesto upon the subject of non-combatants. He could recognise his own handwriting across the room. The Major saw it too.

"Hallo, what's that hanging up, I wonder?" he exclaimed. "A memorandum for me, I expect; probably from my old friend 'Dados.' [1] Let us get a little more light."

He crossed to the window and drew up the blind. Cockerell moved too. When the Major turned round, his guest was standing by the stove, his face scarlet through its grime.

[1] D.A.D.O.S. Deputy Assistant Director of Ordnance Stores.

"I'm awfully sorry, sir," said Cockerell, "but that notice — memorandum — of yours has dropped into the fire."

"If it came from Dados," replied the Major, "thank you very much!"

"I can't tell you, sir," added Cockerell humbly, "what a fool I feel."

But the apology referred to an entirely different matter.

IX

I

IT is just one year to-day since we "came oot."
A year plays havoc with the "establishment" of
a battalion in these days of civilised warfare. Of
the original band of stout-hearted but inexperienced Crusaders who crossed the Channel in the
van of The First Hundred Thousand, in May,
1915, — a regiment close on a thousand strong,
with twenty-eight officers, — barely two hundred remain, and most of these are Headquarters
or Transport men. Of officers there are five —
Colonel Kemp, Major Wagstaffe, Master Cockerell, Bobby Little, and Mr. Waddell, who, by
the way, is now Captain Waddell, having succeeded to the command of his old Company.

Of the rest, our old Colonel is in Scotland, es-
saying ambitious pedestrian and equestrian feats
upon his new leg. Others have been drafted to
the command of newer units, for every member of
"K (1)" is a Nestor now. Others are home, in
various stages of convalescence. Others, alas! will
never go home again. But the gaps have all been
filled up, and once more we are at full strength,
comfortably conscious that whereas a year ago we
were fighting to hold a line, and play for time, and
find our feet, while the people at home behind us
were making good, now we are fighting for one

thing and one thing only; and that is, to administer the knock-out blow to Brother Boche.

Our last casualty was Ayling, who left us under somewhat unusual circumstances.

Towards the end of our last occupancy of trenches the local Olympus decided that what both sides required, in order to awaken them from their winter lethargy, or spring lassitude (or whatever it is that Olympus considers that we in the firing-line are suffering from for the moment), was a tonic. Accordingly orders were issued for a Flying Matinée, or trench raid. Each battalion in the Division was to submit a scheme, and the battalion whose scheme was adjudged the best was to be accorded the honour — so said the Practical Joke Department — of carrying out the scheme in person. To the modified rapture of the Seventh Hairy Jocks their plan was awarded first prize. Headquarters, after a little excusable recrimination on the subject of unnecessary zeal and misguided ambition, set to work to arrange rehearsals of our highly unpopular production.

Brother Boche has grown "wise" to Flying Matinées nowadays, and to score a real success you have to present him with something comparatively novel and unexpected. However, our scheme had been carefully thought out; and, given sufficient preparation, and an adequate cast, there seemed no reason to doubt that the piece would have a highly successful run of one night.

At one point in the enemy's trenches opposite to us his barbed-wire defences had worn very thin, and steps were taken by means of systematic machine-gun fire to prevent him repairing them. This spot was selected for the raid. A party of twenty-five was detailed. It was to be led by Angus M'Lachlan, and was to slip over the parapet on a given moonless night, crawl across No Man's Land to within striking distance of the German trench, and wait. At a given moment the signal for attack would be given, and the wire demolished by a means which need not be specified here. Thereupon the raiding party were to dash forward and — to quote the Sergeant-Major — "mix themselves up in it."

Two elements are indispensable in a successful trench-raid — surprise and despatch. That is to say, you must deliver your raid when and where it is least expected, and then get home to bed before your victims have had time to set the machinery of retaliation in motion. Steps were therefore taken, firstly, to divert the enemy's attention as far as possible from the true objective of the raid, by a sudden and furious bombardment of a sector of trenches three hundred yards away; and secondly, to ensure as far as possible, that the raid, having commenced at 2 A.M., should conclude at 2.12, sharp.

In order to cover the retirement of the excursionists, Ayling was ordered to arrange for machine-gun fire, which should sweep the enemy's parapet for some hundreds of yards upon either flank, and so encourage the enemy to keep his head down and mind his own business.

The raid itself was a brilliant success. Dug-outs were bombed, emplacements destroyed, and a respectable bag of captives brought over. But the element of surprise, upon which so much insistence was laid above, was visited upon both attackers and attacked. To the former the contribution came from that well-meaning but somewhat addlepated warrior, Private Nigg, who formed one of the raiding party.

Nigg's allotted task upon this occasion was to "comb out" certain German dug-outs. (It may be mentioned that each man had a specific duty to perform, and a specific portion of the trench opposite to perform it in; for the raid had been rehearsed several times in a dummy trench behind the lines constructed exactly to scale from an aeroplane photograph.) For this purpose he was provided with bombs. Shortly before two o'clock in the morning the party, headed by Angus M'Lachlan, crawled over the parapet during a brief lull in the activities of the Verey lights, and crept steadily, on hands and knees, across No Man's Land. Fifty yards from the enemy's wire was a collection of shell-holes, relics of a burst of misdirected energy on the part of a six-inch battery. Here the raiders disposed themselves, and waited for the signal.

Now, it is an undoubted fact, that if you curl yourself up, with two or three preliminary twirls, after the fashion of a dog going to bed, in a perfectly circular shell-hole, on a night as black as the inside of the dog in question, you are extremely likely to lose your sense of direction. This is what happened to Private Nigg. He and

his infernal machines lay uneasily in their appointed shell-hole for some ten minutes, surrounded by Verey lights which shot suddenly into
the sky with a disconcerting *plop*, described a
graceful parabola, burst into dazzling flame, and
fluttered sizzling down. One or two of these fell
quite near Nigg's party, and continued to burn
upon the ground, but the raiders sank closer into
their shell-holes, and no alarm resulted. Once or
twice a machine-gun had a scolding fit, and bullets whispered overhead. But, on the whole, the
night was quiet.

Then suddenly, with a shattering roar, the
feint-artillery bombardment broke forth. Simultaneously word was passed along the raiding line
to stand by. Next moment Angus M'Lachlan
and his followers rose to their feet in the black
darkness, scrambled out of their nests, and
dashed forward to the accomplishment of their
mission.

When Nigg, who had paused a moment to col-
lect his bombs, sprang out of his shell-hole, not a
colleague was in sight. At least, Nigg could see
no one. However, want of courage was not one of
his failings. He bounded blindly forward by himself.

Try as he would he could not overtake the raiding party. However, this mattered little, for suddenly a parapet loomed before him. In this same
parapet, low down, Nigg beheld a black and gaping aperture — plainly a loophole of some kind.

Without a moment's hesitation, Nigg hurled a
Mills grenade straight through the loophole, and

then with one wild screech of "Come away, boys!"
took a flying leap over the parapet — and landed
in his own trench, in the arms of Corporal Mucklewame.

As already noted, it is difficult, when lying
curled up in a circular shell-hole in the dark, to
maintain a true sense of direction.

So the first-fruits of the raid was Captain Ayling, of the *Emma Gees.* He had stationed himself
in a concrete emplacement in the front line, the
better to "observe" the fire of his guns when it
should be required. Unfortunately this was the
destination selected by the misguided Niggs for
his first (and as it proved, last) bomb. The raiders came safely back in due course, but by that
time Ayling, liberally (but by a miracle not dangerously) ballasted with assorted scrap-iron, was
on his way to the First Aid Post.

II

At the present moment we are right back at
rest once more, and are being treated with a
consideration, amounting almost to indulgence,
which convinces us that we are being "fattened
up" — to employ the gruesome but expressive
phraseology of the moment — for some particularly strenuous enterprise in the near future.

Well, we are ready. It is nine months since
Loos, and nearly six since we scraped the nightmare mud of Ypres from our boots, *gum, thigh,* for
the last time. Our recent casualties have been
light — our only serious effort of late has been the
recapture of the Kidney Bean — the new drafts

have settled down, and the young officers have been blooded. And above all, victory is in the air. We are going into our next fight with new-born confidence in the powers behind us. Loos was an experimental affair; and though to the humble instruments with which the experiment was made the proceedings were less hilarious than we had anticipated, the results were enormously valuable to a greatly expanded and entirely untried Staff.

"We shall do better this time," said Major Wagstaffe to Bobby Little, as they stood watching the battalion assemble, in workmanlike fashion, for a route-march. "There are just one or two little points which had not occurred to us then. We have grasped them now, I think."

"Such as?"

"Well, you remember we all went into the Loos show without any very lucid idea as to how far we were to go, and where to knock off for the day, so to speak. The result was that the advance of each Division was regulated by the extent to which the German wire in front of it had been cut by our artillery. Ours was well and truly cut, so we penetrated two or three miles. The people on our left never started at all. Lord knows, they tried hard enough. But how could any troops get through thirty feet of uncut wire, enfiladed by machine-guns? The result was that after forty-eight hours' fighting, our whole•attacking front, instead of forming a nice straight line, had bagged out into a series of bays and peninsulas."

"Our crowd was n't even a peninsula," re-

marked Bobby with feeling. "For an hour or so
it was an island!"

"I think you will find that in the next show
we shall go forward, after intensive bombardment,
quite a short distance; then consolidate; then
wait till the *whole* line has come up to its appointed objective; then bombard again; then go
forward another piece; and so on. That will make
it impossible for gaps to ·be created. It will also
give our gunners a chance to cover our advance
continuously. You remember at Loos they lost
us for hours, and dare not fire for fear of hitting
us. In fact, I expect that in battle plans of the
future, instead of the artillery trying to conform
to the movements of the infantry, matters will
be reversed. The guns, after preliminary bombardment, will create a continuous Niagara of
exploding shells upon a given line, marked in
everybody's map, and timed for an exact period,
just beyond the objective; and the infantry will
stroll up into position a comfortable distance behind, reading the time-table, and dig themselves
in. Then the barrage will lift on to the next line.
and we shall toddle forward again. That's the
new plan, Bobby! Close artillery coöperation,
and a series of limited objectives!"

"It sounds all right," agreed Bobby. "We
shall want a good many guns, though, shan't we?"

"We shall. But don't let that worry you. It is
simply raining guns at the Base now. In fact, my
grandmother in the War Office" — this mythical
relative was frequently quoted by Major Wagstaffe, and certainly her information had several

times proved surprisingly correct — "tells me
that by the beginning of next year we shall have
enough guns, of various calibres, to make a continuous line, hub to hub, from one end of our
front to the other."

"Golly!" observed Captain Little, with respectful relish.

"That means," continued Wagstaffe, "that
we shall be able to blow Brother Boche's immediate place of business to bits, and at the same time
take on his artillery with counter-battery work.
Our shell-supply is practically unlimited now;
so when the next push comes, we foot-sloggers
ought to have a more gentlemanly time of it than
we had at Loos and Wipers. And I'll tell you another thing, Bobby. We shall have command of
the air too."

"That will be a pleasant change," remarked
Bobby. "I'm getting tired of putting my fellows
under arrest for rushing out of carefully concealed
positions in order to gape up at Boche planes
going over. Angus M'Lachlan is as bad as any of
them. The fellow —"

"But you have not seen many Boche planes
lately?"

"No. Certainly not so many."

"And the number will grow beautifully less.
Our little friends in the R.F.C. are getting fairly
numerous now, and their machines have been improved out of all knowledge. They are rapidly
assuming the position of top dog. Moreover, the
average Boche does not take kindly to flying. It
is too — too individualistic a job for him. He

likes to work in a bunch with other Boches, where
he can keep step, and maintain dressing, and
mark time if he gets confused. In the air one cannot mark time, and it worries Fritz to death. I
think you will see, in the next unpleasantness,
that we shall be able to maintain our aeroplane
frontier somewhere over the enemy third line.
That means that we shall make our own dispositions with a certain degree of privacy, and the
Boche will not. Also, when our big guns get to
work, they will not need to fire blindly, as in the
days of our youth, but will be directed by one of
our R.F.C. lads, humming about in his little bus
above the target, perhaps fifteen miles from the
gun. Hallo, there go the pipes! Tell your men
to fall in."

"The whole business," observed Bobby, as he
struggled into his equipment, "sounds so attractive that I am beginning quite to look forward to
the next show!"

"Don't forget the Boche machine-guns, my
lad," replied Wagstaffe.

"One seldom gets the chance," grumbled
Bobby. "Is there no way of knocking them out?"

"Well —" Wagstaffe looked intensely mysterious — "of course one never knows, but — have
you heard any rumours on the subject?"

"I have. About —"

"About the Hush! Hush! Brigade?"

Bobby nodded.

"Yes," he said. "Young Osborne, my best
subaltern after Angus, disappeared last month to
join it. Tell me, what *is* the —"

"Hush! Hush!" said Major Wagstaffe. "*Mé-
fiez vous! Taisez vous!* and so on!"

The battalion moved off.

So much for the war-talk of veterans. Now let
us listen to the novices.

"Bogle," said Angus M'Lachlan to his henchman, "I think we shall have to lighten this
Wolseley valise of mine. With one thing and another it weighs far more than thirty-five pounds."

"That's a fact, sirr," agreed Mr. Bogle. "It
carries ower mony books in the heid of it."

They shook out the contents of the valise upon
the floor of Angus's bedroom — a loft over the
kitchen in "A" Company's farm billet — and proceeded to prune Angus's personal effects. There
were boots, socks, shaving-tackle, maps, packets
of chocolate, and books of every size, but chiefly
of the ever-blessed sevenpenny type.

"A lot of these things will have to go, Bogle,"
said Angus regretfully. "The colonel has warned
officers about their kits, and it would never do to
have mine turned back from the waggon at the
last minute."

Mr. Bogle pricked up his ears. "The waggon?
Are we for off again, sirr?" he inquired.

"Indeed I could not say," replied the cautious
Angus; "but it is well to be ready."

"The boys was saying, sirr," observed Bogle
tentatively, "that there was to be another grand
battle soon."

"It is more than likely," said Angus, with an
air of profound wisdom. "Here we are in June,

and we must take the offensive, sooner or later, or summer will be over."

"What kind o' a battle will it be this time, sirr?" inquired Bogle respectfully.

"Oh, our artillery will pound the German trenches for a week or two, and then we shall go over the parapet and drive them back for miles," said Angus simply.

"And what then, sirr?"

"What then? We shall go on pushing them until another Division relieves us."

Bogle nodded comprehendingly. He now had firmly fixed in his mind the essential details of the projected great offensive of 1916. He was not interested to go further in the matter. And it is this very faculty — philosophic trust, coupled with absolute lack of imagination — which makes the British soldier the most invincible person in the world. The Frenchman is inspired to glorious deeds by his great spirit and passionate love of his own sacred soil; the German fights as he thinks, like a machine. But the British Tommy wins through owing to his entire indifference to the pros and cons of the tactical situation. He settles down to war like any other trade, and, as in time of peace, he is chiefly concerned with his holidays and his creature comforts. A battle is a mere incident between one set of billets and another. Consequently he does not allow the grim realities of war to obsess his mind when off duty. One might almost ascribe his success as a soldier to the fact that his domestic instincts are stronger than his military instincts.

Put the average Tommy into a trench under fire how does he comport himself? Does he begin by striking an attitude and hurling defiance at the foe? No, he begins by inquiring, in no uncertain voice, where his — dinner is? He then examines his new quarters. Before him stands a parapet, buttressed mayhap with hurdles or balks of timber, the whole being designed to preserve his life from hostile projectiles. How does he treat this bulwark? Unless closely watched, he will begin to chop it up for firewood. His next proceeding is to construct for himself a place of shelter. This sounds a sensible proceeding, but here again it is a case of "safety second." A British Tommy regards himself as completely protected from the assaults of his enemies if he can lay a sheet of corrugated-iron roofing across his bit of trench and sit underneath it. At any rate it keeps the rain off, and that is all that his instincts demand of him. An ounce of comfort is worth a pound of security.

He looks about him. The parapet here requires fresh sandbags; there the trench needs pumping out. Does he fill sandbags, or pump, of his own volition? Not at all. Unless remorselessly supervised, he will devote the rest of the morning to inventing and chalking up a title for his new dugout — "Jock's Lodge," or "Burns' Cottage," or "Cyclists' Rest" — supplemented by a cautionary notice, such as — *No Admittance. This Means You.* Thereafter, with shells whistling over his head, he will decorate the parapet in his immediate vicinity with picture postcards and

cigarette photographs. Then he leans back with
a happy sigh. His work is done. His home from
home is furnished. He is now at leisure to think
about "they Gairmans" again. That may sound
like an exaggeration; but "Comfort First" is the
motto of that lovable but imprudent grasshopper,
Thomas Atkins, all the time.

A sudden and pertinent thought occurred to
Mr. Bogle, who possessed a Martha-like nature.

"What way, sir, will a body get his dinner, if
we are to be fighting for twa-three days on end?"

"Every man," replied Angus, "will be issued,
I expect, with two days' rations. But the Colonel
tells me that during hard fighting a man does not
feel the desire for food — or sleep either for that
matter. Perhaps, during a lull, it may occur to
him that he has not eaten since yesterday, and he
may pull out a bit of biscuit or chocolate from his
pocket, just to nibble. Or he may remember that
he has had no sleep for twenty-four hours — so he
just drops down and sleeps for ten minutes while
there is time. But generally, matters of ordinary
routine drop out of a man's thoughts altogether."

"That's a queer-like thing, a body forgetting
his dinner!" murmured Bogle.

"Of course," continued Angus, warming to his
theme like his own father in his pulpit, "if Nature
is expelled with a pitchfork in this manner, for too
long, *tamen usque recurret.*"

"Is that a fact?" replied Bogle politely. He
always adopted the line of least resistance when
his master took to audible rumination. "Weel,
I'll hae to be steppin', sir. I'll pit these twa

blankets oot in the sun, in some place where the
dooks frae the pond will no get dandering ower
them. And if you'll sorrt your books, I'll hand
ower the yins ye dinna require to the Y.M.C.A.
hut ayont the village."

Bogle cherished a profound admiration for
Lieutenant M'Lachlan both as a scholar and a
strategist, and absorbed his deliverances with a
care and attention which enabled him to misquote
the same quite fluently to his own associates.
That very evening he set forth the coming plan
of campaign, as elucidated to him by his master,
to a mixed assemblage at the *Estaminet au Clef
des Champs*. Some of the party were duly impressed; but Mr. Spike Johnson, a resident in
peaceful times of Stratford-atte-Bow, the recognised humourist of the Sappers' Field Company
attached to the Brigade, was pleased to be facetious.

"It won't be no good you Jocks goin' over no
parapet to attack no 'Uns," he said, "after what
'appened last week!"

This dark saying had the effect of rousing every
Scottish soldier in the *estaminet* to a state of
bristling attention.

"And what was it," inquired Private Cosh with
heat, "that happened last week?"

"Why," replied Mr. Johnson, who had been
compounding this jest for some days, and now
saw his opportunity to deliver it with effect at
short range, "your trenches got raided last
Wednesday, when you was in 'em. By the
Brandyburgers, I think it was."

The entire symposium stared at the jester with undisguised amazement.

"Our — trenches," proclaimed Private Tosh with forced calm, "were never raided by no — Brandyburrrgerrs! Was they, Jimmie?"

Mr. Cosh corroborated, with three adjectives which Mr. Tosh had not thought of.

Spike Johnson merely smiled, with the easy assurance of a man who has the ace up his sleeve.

"Oh yes, they was!" he reiterated.

"They werre *not!*" shouted half a dozen voices.

The next stage of the discussion requires no discription. It terminated, at the urgent request of Madame from behind the bar, and with the assistance of the Military Police, in the street outside.

"And now, Spike Johnson," inquired Private Cosh, breathing heavily but much refreshed, "can you tell me what way Gairmans could get intil the trenches of a guid Scots regiment withoot bein' *seen ?*"

"I can," replied Mr. Johnson with relish, "and I will. They got in all right, but you did n't see them, because they was disguised."

Cosh and Tosh snorted disdainfully, and Private Nigg, who was present with his friend Buncle, inquired —

"What way was they disguised?"

Like lightning came the answer —

"*As a joke!* Oh, you Jocks."

Cosh and Tosh (who had already been warned by the Police sergeant) merely glared and gurgled impotently. Private Nigg, who, as already men-

tioned, was slightly wanting in quickness of per-
ception, was led away by the faithful Buncle, to
have the outrage explained to him at leisure. It
was Private Bogle who intervened, and brought
the intellectual Goliath crashing to the ground.

"Man, Johnson," he remarked, and shook his
head mournfully, "youse ought to be varra careful aboot sayin' things like that to the likes of us.
'Deed aye!"

"What for, ole son?" inquired the jester indul-
gently.

"Naithing," replied Bogle with artistic reti-
cence.

"Come along — aht with it!" insisted Johnson.
"Cough it up, duckie!"

"Man, man," cried Bogle with passionate earnestness, "dinna gang ower far!"

"What the 'ell *for?*" inquired Johnson, impressed despite himself.

"What for?" Bogle's voice dropped to a
ghostly whisper. "Has it ever occurred to you,
my mannie, what would happen tae the English
— if Scotland was tae make a separate peace?"

And Mr. Bogle retired, not before it was time,
within the sheltering portals of the *estaminet*,
where not less than seven inarticulate but appreciative fellow-countrymen offered him refreshment.

X

I

An Observation Post — or "O Pip," in the mysterious *patois* of the Buzzers — is not exactly the spot that one would select either for spaciousness or accessibility. It may be situated up a chimney or up a tree, or down a tunnel bored through a hill. But it certainly enables you to see something of your enemy; and that, in modern warfare, is a very rare and valuable privilege.

Of late the scene-painter's art — technically known as *camouflage* — has raised the concealment of batteries and their observation posts to the realm of the uncanny. According to Major Wagstaffe, you can now disguise anybody as anything. For instance, you can make up a battery of six-inch guns to look like a flock of sheep, and herd them into action browsing. Or you can despatch a scouting party across No Man's Land dressed up as pillar-boxes, so that the deluded Hun, instead of opening fire with a machine-gun, will merely post letters in them — valuable letters, containing military secrets. Lastly, and more important still, you can disguise yourself to look like nothing at all, and in these days of intensified artillery fire it is very seldom that nothing at all is hit.

The particular O Pip with which we are con-

cerned at present, however, is a German post —
or was a fortnight ago, before the opening of the
Battle of the Somme.

For nearly two years the British Armies on the
Western Front have been playing for time. They
have been sticking their toes in and holding their
ground, with numerically inferior forces and inadequate artillery support, against a nation in
arms which has set out, with forty years of preparation at its back, to sweep the earth. We have
held them, and now *der Tag* has come for us. The
deal has passed into our hand at last. A fortnight
ago, ready for the first time to undertake the
offensive on a grand and prolonged scale, — Loos
was a mere reconnaissance compared with this,
— the New British Army went over the parapet
shoulder to shoulder with the most heroic Army
in the world — the Army of France — and attacked over a sixteen-mile front in the Valley of
the Somme.

It was a critical day for the Allies: certainly it
was a most critical day in the history of the British Army. For on that day an answer had to be
given to a very big question indeed. Hitherto
we had been fighting on the defensive — unready, uphill, against odds. It would have been
no particular discredit to us had we failed to hold
our line. But we had held it, and more. Now,
at last, we were ready — as ready as we were ever
likely to be. We had the men, the guns, and the
munitions. We were in a position to engage the
enemy on equal, and more than equal, terms.
And the question that the British Empire had to

answer in that day, the First of July 1916, was
this: "Are these new amateur armies of ours,
raised, trained, and equipped in less than two
years, with nothing in the way of military tradition to uphold them — nothing but the steady
courage of their race: are they a match for, and
more than a match for, that grim machine-made,
iron-bound host that lies waiting for them along
that line of Picardy hills? Because if they are *not*,
we cannot win this war. We can only make a
stalemate of it."

We, looking back now over a space of twelve
months, know how our boys answered that question. In the greatest and longest battle that the
world had yet seen, that Army of city clerks,
Midland farm-lads, Lancashire mill-hands, Scottish miners, and Irish corner-boys, side by side
with their great-hearted brethren from Overseas,
stormed positions which had been held impregnable for two years, captured seventy thousand
prisoners, reclaimed several hundred square miles
of the sacred soil of France, and smashed once and
for all the German-fostered fable of the invinci-
bility of the German Army. It was good to have
lived and suffered during those early and lean
years, if only to be present at their fulfilment.

But at this moment the battle was only beginning, and the bulk of their astounding achievement was still to come. Nevertheless, in the
cautious and modest estimate of their Comman-
der-in-Chief, they had already done something.

After ten days and nights of continuous fighting,
said the first official report, *our troops have com-*

pleted the methodical capture of the whole of the
enemy's first system of defence on a front of fourteen
thousand yards. This system of defence consisted of
numerous and continuous lines of fire trenches,
extending to depths of from two thousand to four
thousand yards, and included five strongly fortified
villages, numerous heavily entrenched woods, and a
large number of immensely strong redoubts. The
capture of each of these trenches represented an
operation of some importance, and the whole of them
are now in our hands.

Quite so. One feels, somehow, that Berlin
would have got more out of such a theme.

Now let us get back to our O Pip. If you peep
over the shoulder of Captain Leslie, the gunner
observing officer, as he directs the fire of his
battery, situated some thousands of yards in
rear, through the medium of map, field-glass, and
telephone, you will obtain an excellent view of
to-morrow's field of battle. Present in the O Pip
are Colonel Kemp, Wagstaffe, Bobby Little, and
Angus M'Lachlan. The latter had been included
in the party because, to quote his Commanding
Officer, "he would have burst into tears if he had
been left out."

Overhead roared British shells of every kind
and degree of unpleasantness, for the ground
in front was being "prepared" for the coming
assault. The undulating landscape, running up
to a low ridge on the skyline four miles away, was
spouting smoke in all directions — sometimes
black, sometimes green, and sometimes, where

bursting shell and brick-dust intermingled, blood-
red. Beyond the ridge all-conquering British.
aeroplanes occupied the firmament, observing
for "mother" and "granny" and signalling encouragement or reproof to these ponderous but
sprightly relatives as their shells hit or missed the
target.

"Yes, sir," replied Leslie to Colonel Kemp's
question, "that is Longueval, on the slope opposite, with the road running through on the way to
Flers, over the skyline. That is Delville Wood on
its right. As you see, the guns are concentrating
on both places. That is Waterlot Farm, on this
side of the wood — a sugar refinery. Regular nest
of machine-guns there, I'm told."

"No doubt we shall be able to confirm the
rumour to-morrow," said Colonel Kemp drily.
"That is Bernafay Wood on our right, I suppose?"

"Yes, sir. We hold the whole of that. The
pear-shaped wood out beyond it — it looks as if
it were joined on, but the two are quite separate
really — is Trones Wood. It has changed hands
several times. Just at present I don't think we
hold more than the near end. Further away, half-
right, you can see Guillemont."

"In that case," remarked Wagstaffe, "our
right flank would appear to be strongly supported
by the enemy."

"Yes. We are in a sort of right-angled salient
here. We have the enemy on our front and our
right. In fact, we form the extreme right of the
attacking front. Our left is perfectly secure, as
we now hold Mametz Wood and Contalmaison.

There they are." He waved his glass to the north-
west. "When the attack takes place, I understand that our Division will go straight ahead, for
Longueval and Delville Wood, while the next
Division makes a lateral thrust out to the right,
to push the Boche out of Trones Wood and cover
our flank."

"I believe that is so," said the Colonel.
"Bobby, take a good look at the approaches to
Longueval. That is the scene of to-morrow's
constitutional."

Bobby and Angus obediently scanned the village through their glasses. Probably they did not
learn much. One bombarded French village is
very like another bombarded French village. A
cowering assemblage of battered little houses;
a pitiful little main street, with its eviscerated
shops and *estaminets;* a shattered church-spire.
Beyond that, an enclosure of splintered stumps
that was once an orchard. Below all, cellars, reinforced with props and sand-bags, and filled with
machine-guns. *Voilà tout!*

Presently the Gunner Captain passed word
down to the telephone operator to order the battery to cease fire.

"Knocking off?" inquired Wagstaffe.

"For the present, yes. We are only registering
this morning. Not all our batteries are going at
once, either. We don't want Brother Boche to
know our strength until we tune up for the final
chorus. We calculate that —"

"There is a comfortable sense of decency and
order about the way we fight nowadays," said

Colonel Kemp. "It is like working out a problem in electrical resistance by a nice convenient algebraical formula. Very different from the state of things last year, when we stuck it out by employing rule of thumb and hanging on by our eyebrows."

"The only problem we can't quite formulate is the machine-gun," said Leslie. The Boche's dugouts here are thirty feet deep. When crumped by our artillery he withdraws his infantry and leaves his machine-gunners behind, safe underground. Then, when our guns lift and the attack comes over, his machine-gunners appear on the surface, hoist their guns after them with a sort of tackle arrangement, and get to work on a prearranged band of fire. The infantry can't do them in until No Man's Land is crossed, and — well, they don't all get across, that's all! However, I *have* heard rumours —"

"So have we all," said Colonel Kemp.

"I forgot to tell you, Colonel," interposed Wagstaffe, "that I met young Osborne at Divisional Headquarters last night. You remember, he left us some time ago to join the Hush! Hush! Brigade."

"I remember," said the Colonel.

By this time the party, including the Gunner Captain, were filing along a communication trench, lately the property of some German gentlemen, on their way back to headquarters.

"Did he tell you anything, Wagstaffe?" continued Colonel Kemp.

"Not much. Apparently the time of the H.H.B.

is not yet. But he made an appointment with me
for this evening — in the gloaming, so to speak.
He is sending a car. If all he says is true, the
Boche *Emma Gee* is booked for an eye-opener in
a few weeks' time."

II

That evening a select party of sight-seers were
driven to a secluded spot behind the battle line.
Here they were met by Master Osborne, obviously inflated with some important matter.

"I've got leave from my C.O. to show you the
sights, sir," he announced to Colonel Kemp. "If
you will all stand here and watch that wood on
the opposite side of this clearing, you may see
something. We don't show ourselves much except
in late evening, so this is our parade hour."

The little group took up its appointed stand
and waited in the gathering ₁dusk. In the east
the sky was already twinkling with intermittent
Verey lights. All around the British guns were
thundering forth their hymns of hate — full-
throated now, for the hour for the next great
assault was approaching.

Wagstaffe's thoughts went back to a certain
soft September night last year, when he and
Blaikie had stood on the eastern outskirts of
Bethune listening to a similar overture — the
prelude to the Battle of Loos. But this overture
was ten times more awful, and, from a material
British point of view, ten times more inspiring.
It would have thrilled old Blaikie's fighting
spirit, thought Wagstaffe. But Loos had taken

his friend from him, and he, Wagstaffe, only was
left. What did fate hold in store for him to-morrow? he wondered. And Bobby? They had both
escaped marvellously so far. Well, better men
had gone before them. Perhaps —

Fingers of steel bit into his biceps muscle, and
the excited whinny of Angus M'Lachlan besought
him to look!

Down in the forest something stirred. But it was
not the note of a bird, as the song would have us
believe. From the depths of the wood opposite
came a crackling, crunching sound, as of some
prehistoric beast forcing its way through tropical
undergrowth. And then, suddenly, out from the
thinning edge there loomed a monster — a mon-
strosity. It did not glide, it did not walk. It
wallowed. It lurched, with now and then a laborious heave of its shoulders. It fumbled its way
over a low bank matted with scrub. It crossed a
ditch, by the simple expedient of rolling the ditch
out flat, and waddled forward. In its path stood
a young tree. The monster arrived at the tree
and laid its chin lovingly against the stem. The
tree leaned back, crackled, and assumed a hori-
zontal position. In the middle of the clearing,
twenty yards farther on, gaped an enormous shell-
crater, a present from the Kaiser. Into this the
creature plunged blindly, to emerge, panting and
puffing, on the farther side. Then it stopped. A
magic opening appeared in its stomach, from
which emerged, grinning, a British subaltern and
his grimy associates.

And that was our friends' first encounter with

a "Tank." The secret — unlike most secrets in this publicity-ridden war — had been faithfully kept; so far the Hush! Hush! Brigade had been little more than a legend even to the men high up. Certainly the omniscient Hun received the surprise of his life when, in the early mist of a September morning some weeks later, a line of these selfsame tanks burst for the first time upon his incredulous vision, waddling grotesquely up the hill to the ridge which had defied the British infantry so long and so bloodily — there to squat complacently down on the top of the enemy's machine-guns, or spout destruction from her own up and down beautiful trenches which had never been intended for capture. In fact, Brother Boche was quite plaintive about the matter. He described the employment of such engines as wicked and brutal, and opposed to the recognised usages of warfare. When one of these low-comedy vehicles (named the *Crême-de-Menthe*) ambled down the main street of the hitherto impregnable village of Flers, with hysterical British Tommies slapping her on the back, he appealed to the civilised world to step in and forbid the combination of vulgarism and barbarity.

"Let us at least fight like gentlemen," said the Hun, with simple dignity. "Let us stick to legitimate military devices — the murder of women and children, and the emission of chlorine gas. But Tanks—no! One must draw the line somewhere!"

But the ill-bred *Crême-de-Menthe* took no notice. None whatever. She simply went waddling on — towards Berlin.

"An experiment, of course," commented Colonel Kemp, as they returned to headquarters — "a fantastic experiment. But I wish they were ready now. I would give something to see one of them leading the way into action to-morrow. It might mean saving the lives of a good many of my boys."

XI

THE LAST SOLO

It was dawn on Saturday morning, and the second phase of the Battle of the Somme was more than twenty-four hours old. The programme had opened with a night attack, always the most difficult and uncertain of enterprises, especially for soldiers who were civilians less than two years ago. But no undertaking is too audacious for men in whose veins the wine of success is beginning to throb. And this undertaking, this hazardous gamble, had succeeded all along the line. During the past day and night, more than three miles of the German second system of defences, from Bazentin le Petit to the edge of Delville Wood, had received their new tenants; and already long streams of not altogether reluctant Hun prisoners were being escorted to the rear by perspiring but cheerful gentlemen with fixed bayonets.

Meanwhile — in case such of the late occupants of the line as were still at large should take a fancy to revisit their previous haunts, working-parties of infantry, pioneers, and sappers were toiling at full pressure to reverse the parapets, run out barbed wire, and bestow machine-guns in such a manner as to produce a continuous lattice-work of fire along the front of the captured position.

All through the night the work had continued. As a result, positions were now tolerably secure, the intrepid "Buzzers" had included the newly grafted territory in the nervous system of the British Expeditionary Force, and Battalion Headquarters and Supply Dépôts had moved up to their new positions.

To Colonel Kemp and his Adjutant Cockerell, ensconced in a dug-out thirty feet deep, furnished with a real bed, electric-light fittings, and ornaments obviously made in Germany, entered Major Wagstaffe, encrusted with mud, but as imperturbable as ever. He saluted.

"Good-morning, sir. You seem to have struck a cushie little home time."

"Yes. The Boche officer harbours no false modesty about acknowledging his desire for creature comforts. That is where he scores off people like you and me, who pretend we like sleeping in mud. Have you been round the advanced positions?"

"Yes. There is some pretty hard fighting going on in the village itself — the Boche still holds the north-west corner — and in the wood on the right. 'A' Company are holding a line of broken-down cottages on our right front, but they can't make any further move until they get more bombs. The Boche is occupying various buildings opposite, but in no great strength at present. However, he seems to have plenty of machine-guns."

"I have sent up more bombs," said the Colonel. "What about 'B' Company?"

"'B' have reached their objective, and consolidated. 'C' and 'D' are lying close up, ready to go forward in support when required. I think 'A' could do with a little assistance."

"I don't want to send up 'C' and 'D'," replied the Colonel, "until the Divisional Reserve arrives. The Brigade has just telephoned through that reinforcements are on the way. When they get here, we can afford to stuff in the whole battalion. Are 'A' Company capable of handling the situation at present?"

"Yes, I think so. Little is directing his platoons from a convenient cellar. He was in touch with them all when I left. But it is possible that the Boche may make a rush when it grows a bit lighter. At present he is too demoralised to attempt anything beyond intermittent machine-gun fire."

Colonel Kemp turned to Cockerell.

"Get Captain Little on the telephone," he said, "and tell him, if the enemy displays any disposition to counter-attack, to let me know at once." Then he turned to Wagstaffe, and asked the question which always lurks furtively on the tongue of a commanding officer.

"Many — casualties?"

"'A' Company have caught it rather badly crossing the open. 'B' got off lightly. Glen is commanding them now: Waddell was killed leading his men in the rush to the final objective."

Colonel Kemp sighed.

"Another good boy gone — veteran, rather. I must write to his wife. Fairly newly married, I fancy?"

"Four months," said Wagstaffe briefly.

"What was his Christian name, do you know?"

"Walter, I think, sir," said Cockerell.

Colonel Kemp, amid the stress of battle, found time to enter a note in his pocket-diary to that effect.

Meanwhile, up in the line, 'A' Company were holding on grimly to what are usually described as "certain advanced elements" of the village.

Village fighting is a confused and untidy business, but it possesses certain redeeming features. The combatants are usually so inextricably mixed up that the artillery are compelled to refrain from participation. That comes later, when you have cleared the village of the enemy, and his guns are preparing the ground for the inevitable counter-attack.

So far 'A' Company had done nobly. From the moment when they had lined up before Montauban in the gross darkness preceding yesterday's dawn until the moment when Bobby Little led them in one victorious rush into the outskirts of the village, they had never encountered a setback. By sunset they had penetrated some way farther; now creeping stealthily forward under the shelter of a broken wall to hurl bombs into the windows of an occupied cottage; now climbing precariously to some commanding position in order to open fire with a Lewis gun; now making a sudden dash across an open space. Such work offered peculiar opportunities to small and well-handled parties — opportunities of which Bobby Little's veterans availed themselves right readily.

Angus M'Lachlan, for instance, accompanied

by a small following of seasoned experts, had twice rounded up parties of the enemy in cellars, and had despatched the same back to Headquarters with his compliments and a promise of more. Mucklewame and four men had bombed their way along a communication trench leading to one of the side streets of the village — a likely avenue for a counter-attack — and having reached the end of the trench, had built up a sandbag barricade, and had held the same against the assaults of hostile bombers until a Vickers machine-gun had arrived in charge of an energetic subaltern of that youthful but thriving organisation, the Suicide Club, or Machine-Gun Corps, and closed the street to further Teutonic traffic.

During the night there had been periods of quiescence, devoted to consolidation, and here and there to snatches of uneasy slumber. Angus M'Lachlan, fairly in his element, had trailed his enormous length in and out of the back-yards and brick-heaps of the village, visiting every point in his irregular line, testing defences; bestowing praise; and ensuring that every man had his share of food and rest. Unutterably grimy but inexpressibly cheerful, he reported progress to Major Wagstaffe when that nocturnal rambler visited him in the small hours.

"Well, Angus, how goes it?" inquired Wagstaffe.

"We have won the match, sir," replied Angus with simple seriousness. "We are just playing the bye now!"

And with that he crawled away, with the

unnecessary stealth of a small boy playing rob-
bers, to encourage his dour paladins to further
efforts.

"We shall probably be relieved this evening,"
he explained to them, "and we must make everything secure. It would never do to leave our new
positions untenable by other troops. They might
not be so reliable" — with a paternal smile —
"as you! Now, our right flank is not safe yet.
We can improve the position very much if we
can secure that *estaminet*, standing up like an
island among those ruined houses on our right
front. You see the sign, *Aux Bons Fermiers*, over
the door. The trouble is that a German machine-
gun is sweeping the intervening space — and we
cannot see the gun! There it goes again. See the
brick-dust fly! Keep down! They are firing
mainly across our front, but a stray bullet may
come this way."

The platoon crouched low behind their improvised rampart of brick rubble, while machine-gun
bullets swept low, with misleading *claquement*,
along the space in front of them, from some hid-
den position on their right. Presently the firing
stopped. Brother Boche was merely "loosing off
a belt," as a precautionary measure, at commend-
ably regular intervals.

"I cannot locate that gun," said Angus impa-
tiently. "Can you, Corporal M'Snape?"

"It is not in the estamint itself, sirr," replied
M'Snape. ("Estamint" is as near as our rank
and file ever get to *estaminet*.) "It seems to be
mounted some place higher up the street. I doubt

they cannot see us themselves — only the ground in front of us."

"If we could reach the *estaminet* itself," said Angus thoughtfully, "we could get a more extended view. Sergeant Mucklewame, select ten men, including three bombers, and follow me. I am going to find a jumping-off place. The Lewis gun too."

Presently the little party were crouching round their officer in a sheltered position on the right of the line — which for the moment appeared to be "in the air." Except for the intermittent streams of machine-gun fire, and an occasional shrapnel-burst overhead, all was quiet. The enemy's counter-attack was not yet ready.

"Now listen carefully," said Angus, who had just finished scribbling a despatch. "First of all, you, Bogle, take this message to the telephone, and get it sent to Company Headquarters. Now you others. We will wait till that machine-gun has fired another belt. Then, the moment it has finished, while they are getting out the next belt, I will dash across to the *estaminet* over there. M'Snape, you will come with me, but no one else — yet. If the *estaminet* seems capable of being held, I will signal to you, Sergeant Mucklewame, and you will send your party across, in driblets, not forgetting the Lewis gun. By that time I may have located the German machine-gun, so we should be able to knock it out with the Lewis."

Further speech was cut short by a punctual fantasia from the gun in question. Angus and

M'Snape crouched behind the shattered wall, awaiting their chance. The firing ceased.

"*Now!*" whispered Angus.

Next moment officer and corporal were flying across the open, and before the mechanical Boche gunner could jerk the new belt into position, both had found sanctuary within the open doorway of the half-ruined *estaminet*.

Nay, more than both; for as the panting pair flung themselves into shelter, a third figure, short and stout, in an ill-fitting kilt, tumbled heavily through the doorway after them. Simultaneously a stream of machine-gun bullets went storming past.

"Just in time!" observed Angus, well pleased. "Bogle, what are you doing here?"

"I was given tae unnerstand, sirr," replied Mr. Bogle calmly, "when I jined the regiment, that in action an officer's servant stands by his officer."

"That is true," conceded Angus; "but you had no right to follow me against orders. Did you not hear me say that no one but Corporal M'Snape was to come?"

"No, sirr. I doubt I was away at the 'phone."

"Well, now you are here, wait inside this doorway, where you can see Sergeant Mucklewame's party, and look out for signals. M'Snape, let us find that machine-gun."

The pair made their way to the hitherto blind side of the building, and cautiously peeped through a much-perforated shutter in the living-room.

"Do you see it, sirr?" inquired M'Snape eagerly.

Angus chuckled.

"See it? Fine! It is right in the open, in the middle of the street. Look!"

He relinquished his peep-hole. The German machine-gun was mounted in the street itself, behind an improvised barrier of bricks and sandbags. It was less than a hundred yards away, sited in a position which, though screened from the view of Angus's platoon farther down, enabled it to sweep all the ground in front of the position. This it was now doing with great intensity, for the brief public appearance of Angus and M'Snape had effectually converted intermittent into continuous fire.

"We must get the Lewis gun over at once," muttered Angus. "It can knock that breastwork to pieces."

He crossed the house again, to see if any of Mucklewame's men had arrived.

They had not. The man with the Lewis gun was lying dead halfway across the street, with his precious weapon on the ground beside him. Two other men, both wounded, were crawling back whence they came, taking what cover they could from the storm of bullets which whizzed a few inches over their flinching bodies.

Angus hastily semaphored to Mucklewame to hold his men in check for the present. Then he returned to the other side of the house.

"How many men are serving that gun?" he said to M'Snape. "Can you see?"

"Only two, sirr, I think. I cannot see them, but that wee breastwork will not cover more than a couple of men."

"Mphm," observed Angus thoughtfully. "I expect they have been left behind to hold on. Have you a bomb about you?"

The admirable M'Snape produced from his pocket a Mills grenade, and handed it to his superior.

"Just the one, sirr," he said.

"Go you," commanded Angus, his voice rising to a more than usually Highland inflection, "and semaphore to Mucklewame that when he hears the explosion of *this*" — he pulled out the safety-pin of the grenade and gripped the grenade itself in his enormous paw —"followed, probably, by the temporary cessation of the machine-gun, he is to bring his men over here in a bunch, as hard as they can pelt. Put it as briefly as you can, but make sure he understands. He has a good signaller with him. Send Bogle to report when you have finished. Now repeat what I have said to you. . . . That's right. Carry on!"

M'Snape was gone. Angus, left alone, pensively restored the safety-pin to the grenade, and laid the grenade upon the ground beside him. Then he proceeded to write a brief letter in his field message-book. This he placed in an envelope which he took from his breast pocket. The envelope was already addressed — to the *Reverend Neil M'Lachlan, The Manse*, in a very remote Highland village. (Angus had no mother.) He closed the envelope, initialled it, and buttoned it up in his breast pocket again. After that he took up his grenade and proceeded to make a further examination of the premises. Presently he found what he wanted; and by the time Bogle arrived to announce that Sergeant Mucklewame had signalled "message understood," his arrangements were complete.

"Stay by this small hole in the wall, Bogle," he said, "and the moment the Lewis gun arrives tell them to mount it here and open fire on the enemy gun."

He left the room, leaving Bogle alone, to listen to the melancholy rustle of peeling wall-paper within and the steady crackling of bullets without. But when, peering through the improvised loop-hole, he next caught sight of his officer, Angus had emerged from the house by the cellar window, and was creeping with infinite caution behind the shelter of what had once been the wall of the *estaminet's* back-yard (but was now an uneven bank of bricks, averaging two feet high), in the direction of the German machine-gun. The gun, oblivious of the danger now threatening its right front, continued to fire steadily and hopefully down the street.

Slowly, painfully, Angus crawled on, until he found himself within the right angle formed by the corner of the yard. He could go no further without being seen. Between him and the German gun lay the cobbled surface of the street, offering no cover whatsoever except one mighty shell-crater, situated midway between Angus and the gun, and full to the brim with rainwater.

A single peep over the wall gave him his bearings. The gun was too far away to be reached by a grenade, even when thrown by Angus M'Lachlan. Still, it would create a diversion. It was a time bomb. He would —

He stretched out his long arm to its full extent behind him, gave one mighty overarm sweep, and with all the crackling strength of his mighty sinews, hurled the grenade.

It fell into the exact centre of the flooded shell-crater.

Angus said something under his breath which would have shocked a disciple of Kultur. Fortunately the two German gunners did not hear him. But they observed the splash fifty yards away, and it relieved them from *ennui*, for they were growing tired of firing at nothing. They had not seen the grenade thrown, and were a little puzzled as to the cause of the phenomenon.

Four seconds later their curiosity was more than satisfied. With a muffled roar, the shell-hole suddenly spouted its liquid contents and other *débris* straight to the heavens, startling them considerably and entirely obscuring their vision.

A moment later, with an exultant yell, Angus M'Lachlan was upon them. He sprang into their vision out of the descending cascade — a towering, terrible, kilted figure, bare-headed and Berserk mad. He was barely forty yards away.

Initiative is not the *forte* of the Teuton. Number One of the German gun mechanically traversed his weapon four degrees to the right and continued to press the thumb-piece. Mud and

splinters of brick sprang up round Angus's feet;
but still he came on. He was not twenty yards
away now. The gunner, beginning to boggle between waiting and bolting, fumbled at his ele-
vating gear, but Angus was right on him before
his thumbs got back to work. Then indeed the
gun spoke out with no uncertain voice, for perhaps two seconds. After that it ceased fire altogether.

Almost simultaneously there came a triumphant roar lower down the street, as Mucklewame
and his followers dashed obliquely across into the
estaminet. Mucklewame himself was carrying the
derelict Lewis gun. In the doorway stood the
watchful M'Snape.

"This way, quick!" he shouted. "We have the
Gairman gun spotted, and the officer is needing
the Lewis!"

But M'Snape was wrong. The Lewis was not
required.

A few moments later, in the face of brisk snip-
ing from the houses higher up the street, James
Bogle, officer's servant, — a member of that de-
spised class which, according to the *Bandar-log*
at home, spend the whole of its time pressing
its master's trousers and smoking his cigarettes
somewhere back in billets, — led out a stretcher
party to the German gun. Number One had been
killed by a shot from Angus's revolver. Number Two had adopted Hindenburg tactics, and
was no more to be seen. Angus himself was
lying, stone dead, a yard from the muzzle of

the gun which he, single-handed, had put out of action.

His men carried him back to the *Estaminet aux Bons Fermiers*, with the German gun, which was afterwards employed to good purpose during the desperate days of attacking and counter-attacking which ensued before the village was finally secured. They laid him in the inner room, and proceeded to put the *estaminet* in a state of defence — ready to hold the same against all comers until such time as the relieving Division should take over, and they themselves be enabled, under the kindly cloak of darkness, to carry back their beloved officer to a more worthy resting-place.

In the left-hand breast pocket of Angus's tunic they found his last letter to his father. Two German machine-gun bullets had passed through it. It was forwarded with a covering letter, by Colonel Kemp. In the letter Angus's commanding officer informed Neil M'Lachlan that his son had been recommended posthumously for the highest honour that the King bestows upon his soldiers.

But for the moment Mucklewame's little band had other work to occupy them. Shelling had recommenced; the enemy were mustering in force behind the village; and presently a series of counter-attacks were launched. They were successfully repelled, in the first instance by the remainder of "A" Company, led in person by Bobby Little, and, when the final struggle came, by the Battalion Reserve under Major Wagstaffe.

And throughout the whole grim struggle which ensued, the *Estaminet aux Bons Fermiers*, tenanted by some of our oldest friends, proved itself the head and corner of the successful defence.

XII

I

Two steamers lie at opposite sides of the dock. One is painted a most austere and unobtrusive grey; she is obviously a vessel with no desire to advertise her presence on the high seas. In other words, a transport. The other is dazzling white, ornamented with a good deal of green, supplemented by red. She makes an attractive picture in the early morning sun. Even by night you could not miss her, for she goes about her business with her entire hull outlined in red lights, regatta fashion, with a great luminous Red Cross blazing on either counter. Not even the Commander of a U-boat could mistake her for anything but what she is — a hospital ship.

First, let us walk round to where the grey ship is discharging her cargo. The said cargo consists of about a thousand unwounded German prisoners.

With every desire to be generous to a fallen foe, it is quite impossible to describe them as a prepossessing lot. Not one man walks like a soldier; they shamble. Naturally, they are dirty and unshaven. So are the wounded men on the white ship: but their outstanding characteristic is an invincible humanity. Beneath the mud and blood they are men — white men. But this strange throng are grey — like their ship. With their shifty eyes and curiously shaped heads, they look like nothing human. They move like over-driven beasts. We realise now why it is that the German Army has to attack in mass.

They pass down the gangway, and are shep-hered into form in the dock shed by the Embarka-tion Staff, with exactly the same silent briskness that characterises the R.A.M.C., over the way. Their guard, with fixed bayonets, exhibit no more or no less concern over them than over half-a-dozen Monday morning malefactors paraded for Orderly Room. Presently they will move off, pos-sibly through the streets of the town; probably they will pass by folk against whose kith and kin they have employed every dirty trick possible in warfare. But there will be no demonstration: there never has been. As a nation we possess a certain number of faults, on which we like to dwell. But we have one virtue at least — we possess a certain sense of proportion; and we are not disposed to make subordinates suffer because we cannot, as yet, get at the principals.

They make a good haul. Fifteen German regi-ments are here represented — possibly more, for some have torn off their shoulder-straps to avoid identification. Some of the units are thinly rep-resented; others more generously. One famous Prussian regiment appears to have thrown its hand in to the extent of about five hundred.

Still, as they stand there, filthy, forlorn, and dazed, one suddenly realises the extreme appro-priateness of a certain reference in the Litany to All Prisoners and Captives.

II

We turn to the hospital ship.

Two great 'brows,' or covered gangways, connect her with her native land. Down these the stretchers are beginning to pass, having been raised from below decks by cunning mechanical devices which cause no jar; and are being conveyed into the cool shade of the dock-shed. Here they are laid in neat rows upon the platform, ready for transfer to the waiting hospital train. Everything is a miracle of quietness and order. The curious public are afar off, held aloof by dock-gates. (They are there in force to-day, partly to cheer the hospital trains as they pass out, partly for reasons connected with the grey-painted ship.) In the dock-shed, organisation and method reign supreme. The work has been going on without intermission for several days and nights; and still the great ships come. The Austurias is outside, waiting for a place at the dock. The Lanfranc is half-way across the English Channel; and there are rumours that the mighty Britannic [1] has selected this, the busiest moment in the opening fortnight of the Somme Battle, to arrive with a miscellaneous and irrelevant cargo of sick and wounded from the Mediterranean. But there is no fuss. The R.A.M.C. Staff Officers, unruffled and cheery, control everything, apparently by a crook of the finger. The stretcher-bearers do their work with silent aplomb.

[1] These three hospital ships were all subsequently sunk by German submarines.

The occupants of the stretchers possess the almost universal feature of a six days' beard — always excepting those who are of an age which is not troubled by such manly accretions. They lie very still — not with the stillness of exhaustion or dejection, but with the comfortable resignation of men who have made good and have suffered in the process; but who now, with their troubles well behind them, are enduring present discomfort under the sustaining prospect of clean beds, chicken diet, and ultimate tea-parties. Such as possess them are wearing Woodbine stumps upon the lower lip.

They are quite ready to compare notes. Let us approach, and listen to a heavily bandaged gentleman who — so the label attached to him informs us — is Private Blank, of the Manchesters, suffering from three "G.S." machine-gun bullet wounds.

"Did the Fritzes run? Yes — they run all right! The last lot saved us trouble by running towards us — with their 'ands up! But their machine-guns — they gave us fair 'Amlet till we got across No Man's Land. After that we used the baynit, and they did n't give us no more vexatiousness. Where did we go in? Oh, near Albert. Our objective was Mary's Court, or some such place." (It is evident that the Battle of the Somme is going to add some fresh household words to our war vocabulary. 'Wipers' is a veteran by this time: 'Plugstreet,' 'Booloo,' and 'Armintears' are old friends. We must now make room for 'Monty Ban,' 'La Bustle,' 'Mucky Farm,' 'Lousy Wood,' and 'Martinpush.')

"What were your prisoners like?"

"'Alf clemmed," said the man from Manchester.

"No rations for three days," explained a Northumberland Fusilier close by. One of his arms was strapped to his side, but the other still clasped to his bosom a German helmet. A British Tommy will cheerfully shed a limb or two in the execution of his duty, but not all the might and majesty of the Royal Army Medical Corps can force him to relinquish a fairly earned 'souvenir.' In fact, owing to certain unworthy suspicions as to the true significance of the initials, "R.A.M.C.," he has been known to refuse chloroform.

"They could n't get nothing up to them for four days, on account of our artillery fire," he added contentedly.

"'Barrage,' my lad!" amended a rather superior person with a lance-corporal's stripe and a bandaged foot.

Indeed, all are unanimous in affirming that our artillery preparation was a tremendous affair. Listen to this group of officers sunning themselves upon the upper deck. They are 'walking cases,' and must remain on board, with what patience they may, until all the 'stretcher cases' have been evacuated.

"Loos was child's play to it," says one — a member of a certain immortal, or at least irrepressible Division which has taken part in every outburst of international unpleasantness since the Marne. "The final hour was absolute pandemonium. And when our new trench-mortar batteries got to work too, — at sixteen to the dozen, — well, it was bad enough for *us;* but what it must have been like at the business end of things, Lord knows! For a few minutes I was almost a pro-Boche!"

Other items of intelligence are gleaned. The weather was 'rotten': mud-caked garments corroborate this statement. The wire, on the whole, was well and truly cut to pieces everywhere; though there were spots at which the enemy contrived to repair it. Finally, ninety per cent of the casualties during the assault were due to machine-gun fire.

But the fact most clearly elicited by casual conversation is this — that the more closely you engage in a battle, the less you know about its progress. This ship is full of officers and men who were in the thick of things for perhaps forty-eight hours on end, but who are quite likely to be utterly ignorant of what was going on round the next traverse in the trench which they had occupied. The wounded Gunners are able to give them a good deal of information. One F.O.O. saw the French advance.

"It was wonderful to see them go in," he said. "Our Batteries were on the extreme right of the British line, so we were actually touching the French left flank. I had met hundreds of *poilus* back in billets, in *cafés*, and the like. To look at them strolling down a village street in their baggy uniforms, with their hands in their pockets, laughing and chatting to the children, you would never

have thought they were such tigers. I remember
one big fellow a few weeks ago, home on leave —
permission — who used to frisk about with a big
umbrella under his arm! I suppose that was to
keep the rain off his tin hat. But when they went
for Maricourt the other day, there were n't many
umbrellas about — only bayonets! .I tell you,
they were marvels!"

It would be interesting to hear the *poilu* on his
Allies.

The first train moves off, and another takes its
place. The long lines of stretchers are thinning
out now. There are perhaps a hundred left.
They contain men of all units — English, Scottish, and Irish. There are Gunners, Sappers, and
Infantry. Here and there among them you may
note bloodstained men in dirty grey uniforms —
men with dull, expressionless faces and closely
cropped heads. They are tended with exactly the
same care as the others. Where wounded men
are concerned, the British Medical Service is
strictly neutral.

A wounded Corporal of the R.A.M.C. turns his
head and gazes thoughtfully at one of those grey
men.

"You understand English, Fritz?" he en-
quires.

Apparently not. Fritz continues to stare woodenly at the roof of the dock-shed.

"I should like to tell 'im a story, Jock," says
the Corporal to his other neighbour. "My job is
on a hospital train. 'Alf-a-dozen 'Un aeroplanes
made a raid behind our lines; and seeing a beauti-

ful Red Cross train — it was a new London and
North Western train, chocolate and white, with
red crosses as plain as could be.— well, they simply could n't resist such a target as that! One of
their machines swooped low down and dropped
his bombs on us. Luckily he only got the rear
coach; but I happened to be in it! D' yer 'ear
that, Fritz?"

"I doot he canna unnerstand onything," remarked the Highlander. "He's fair demoralised,
like the rest. D' ye ken what happened tae me?
I was gaun' back wounded, with *this* —" he indicates an arm strapped close to his side — "and
there was six Fritzes came crawlin' oot o' a dug-
oot, and gave themselves up tae me — *me*, that
was gaun' back wounded, withoot so much as my
jack-knife! Demorralised — that's it!"

"Did you 'ear," enquired a Cockney who came
next in the line, "that all wounded are going to
'ave a nice little gold stripe to wear — a stripe
for every wound?"

There was much interest at this.

"That 'll be fine," observed a man of Kent,
who had been out since Mons, and been wounded
three times. "Folks 'll know now that I'm not
a Derby recruit."

"Where will us wear it?" enquired a gigantic
Yorkshireman, from the next stretcher.

"Wherever you was 'it, lad!" replied the Cockney humourist.

"At that rate," comes the rueful reply, "I shall
'ave to stand oop to show mine!"

III

But now R.A.M.C. orderlies are at hand, and the symposium comes to an end. The stretchers are conveyed one by one into the long open coaches of the train, and each patient is slipped sideways, with gentleness and dispatch, into his appointed cot.

One saloon is entirely filled with officers — the severe cases in the cots, the rest sitting where they can. A newspaper is passed round. There are delighted exclamations, especially from a second lieutenant whose features appear to be held together entirely by strips of plaster. Such parts of the countenance as can be discerned are smiling broadly.

"I *knew* we were doing well," says the bandaged one, devouring the headlines; "but I never knew we were doing as well as this. Official, too! Somme Battle — what? Sorry! I apologise!" as a groan ran round the saloon.

"Never mind," said an unshaven officer, with a twinkling eye, and a major's tunic wrapped loosely around him. "I expect that jest will be overworked by more people than you for the next few weeks. Does anybody happen to know where this train is going to?"

"West of England, somewhere, I believe," replied a voice.

There was an indignant groan from various north countrymen.

"I suppose it is quite impossible to sort us all out at a time like this," remarked a plaintive

Caledonian in an upper cot; "but I fail to see why the R.A.M.C. authorities should go through the mockery of *asking* every man in the train where he wants to be taken, when the train can obviously only go to one place — or perhaps two. I was asked. I said 'Edinburgh'; and the medical wallah said, 'Righto! We'll send you to Bath!'"

"I think I can explain," remarked the wounded major. "These trains usually go to two places — one half to Bath, the other, say, to Exeter. Bath is nearer to Edinburgh than Exeter, so they send you there. It is kindly meant, but —"

"I say," croaked a voice from another cot, — its owner was a young officer who must just have escaped being left behind at a Base hospital as too dangerously wounded to move, — "is that a newspaper down there? Would some one have a look, and tell me if we have got Longueval all right? Longueval? Long — I got pipped, and don't quite —"

The wounded major turned his head quickly.

"Hallo, Bobby!" he observed cheerfully. "That you? I did n't notice you before."

Bobby Little's hot eyes turned slowly on Wagstaffe, and he exclaimed feverishly: —

"Hallo, Major! Cheeroh! Did we stick to Longueval all right? I 've been dreaming about it a bit, and —"

"We did," replied Wagstaffe — "thanks to 'A' Company."

Bobby Little's head fell back on the pillow, and he remarked contentedly: —

"Thanks awfully. I think I can sleep a bit now. So long! See you later!"

His eyes closed, and he sighed happily, as the long train slid out from the platform.

XIII.

THE smoking-room of the Britannia Club used to be exactly like the smoking-room of every other London Club. That is to say, members lounged about in deep chairs, and talked shop, or scandal — or slumbered. At any moment you might touch a convenient bell, and a waiter would appear at your elbow, like a jinnee from a jar, and accept an order with silent deference. You could do this all day, and the jinnee never failed to hear and obey.

That was before the war. Now, those idyllic days are gone. So is the waiter. So is the efficacy of the bell. You may ring, but all that will materialise is a self-righteous little girl, in brass buttons, who will shake her head reprovingly and refer you to certain passages in the Defence of the Realm Act.

Towards the hour of six-thirty, however, something of the old spirit of Liberty asserts itself. A throng of members — chiefly elderly gentlemen in expanded uniforms — assembles in the smoking-room, occupying all the chairs, and even overflowing on to the tables and window-sills. They are not the discursive, argumentative gathering of three years [ago. They sit silent, restless, glancing furtively at their wrist-watches.

The clocks of London strike half-past six. Simultaneously the door of the smoking-room is

thrown open, and a buxom young woman in cap
and apron bounces in. She smiles maternally
upon her fainting flock, and announces: —

"The half-hour's gone. Now you can *all* have
a drink!"

What would have happened if the waiter of old
had done this thing, it is difficult to imagine. But
the elderly gentlemen greet their Hebe with a
chorus of welcome, and clamour for precedence
like children at a school-feast. And yet trusting
wives believe that in his club, at least, a man is
safe!

Major Wagstaffe, D.S.O., having been absent
from London upon urgent public affairs for nearly
three years, was not well versed in the newest refinements of club life. He had arrived that morning from his Convalescent Home in the west
country, and had already experienced a severe
reverse at the hands of the small girl with brass
buttons on venturing to order a sherry and bit-
ters at 11.45 A.M. Consequently, at the statutory
hour, his voice was not uplifted with the rest;
and he was served last. Not least, however; for
Hebe, observing his empty sleeve, poured out his
soda-water with her own fair hands, and offered
to light his cigarette.

This scene of dalliance was interrupted by the
arrival of Captain Bobby Little. He wore the
ribbon of the Military Cross and walked with a
stick — a not unusual combination in these great
days. Wagstaffe made room for him upon the
leather sofa, and Hebe supplied his modest wants
with an indulgent smile.

An autumn and a winter had passed since the attack on Longueval. From July until the December floods, the great battle had raged. The New Armies, supplied at last with abundant munitions, a seasoned Staff, and a concerted plan of action, had answered the question propounded in a previous chapter in no uncertain fashion. Through Longueval and Delville Wood, where the graves of the Highlanders and South Africans now lie thick, through Flers and Martinpuich, through Pozieres and Courcelette, they had fought their way, till they had reached the ridge, with High Wood at its summit, which the Boche, not altogether unreasonably, had regarded as impregnable. The tide had swirled over the crest, down the reverse slope, and up at last to the top of that bloodstained knoll of chalk known as the Butte de Warlencourt. There the Hun threw in his hand. With much loud talk upon the subject of victorious retirements and Hindenburg Lines, he withdrew himself to a region far east of Bapaume; with the result that now some thousand square miles of the soil of France had been restored once and for all to their rightful owners.

But Bobby and Wagstaffe had not been there. All during the autumn and winter they had lain softly in hospital, enjoying their first rest for two years. Wagstaffe had lost his left arm and gained a decoration. Bobby, in addition to his Cross, had incurred a cracked crown and a permanently shortened leg. But both were well content. They had done their bit — and something over; and they had emerged from the din of war with their lives, their health, and their reason. A man who can achieve that feat in this war can count himself fortunate.

Now, passed by a Medical Board as fit for Home Service, they had said farewell to their Convalescent Home and come to London to learn what fate Olympus held in store for them.

"Where have you been all day, Bobby?" enquired Wagstaffe, as they sat down to dinner an hour later.

"Down in Kent," replied Bobby briefly.

"Very well: I will not probe the matter. Been to the War Office?"

"Yes. I was there this morning. I am to be Adjutant of a Cadet school, at Great Snoreham. What sort of a job is that likely to be?"

"On the whole," replied Wagstaffe, "a Fairy Godmother Department job. It might have been very much worse. You are thoroughly up to the Adjutant business, Bobby, and of course the young officers under you will be immensely impressed by your game leg and bit of ribbon. A very sound appointment."

"What are they going to do with you?" asked Bobby in his turn.

"I am to command our Reserve Battalion, with acting rank of Lieutenant-Colonel. Think of that, my lad! They have confirmed you in your rank as Captain, I suppose?"

"Yes."

"Good! The only trouble is that you will be stationed in the South of England and I in the North of Scotland; so we shall not see quite so

much of one another as of late. However, we must
get together occasionally, and split a tin of bully
for old times' sake."

"Bully? By gum!" said Bobby thoughtfully.
"I have almost forgotten what it tastes like.
(Fried sole, please; then roast lamb.) Eight
months in hospital do wash out certain remem-
brances."

"But not all," said Wagstaffè.

"No, not all. I — I wonder how our chaps are
getting on, over there."

"The regiment?"

"Yes. It is so hard to get definite news."

"They were in the Arras show. Did better
than ever; but — well, they required a big draft
afterwards."

"The third time!" sighed Bobby. "Did any
one write to you about it?"

"Yes. Who do you think?"

"Some one in the regiment?"

"Yes."

"I did n't know there were any of the old lot
left. Who was it?"

"Mucklewame."

"Mucklewame? You mean to say the Boche
has n't got *him* yet? It's like missing Rheims
Cathedral."

"Yes, they got him at Arras. Mucklewame is in
hospital. Fortunately his chief wound is in the
head, so he's doing nicely. Here is his letter."

Bobby took the pencilled screed, and read: —

Major Wagstaffe,

*Sir, — I take up my pen for to inform you that I
am now in hospital in Glasgow, having become a
cassuality on the 18th inst.*

*I was struck on the head by the nose-cap of a Ger-
man shell (now in the possession of my guidwife).
Unfortunately I was wearing one of they steel helmets at the time, with the result that I sustained
a serious scalp-wound, also very bad concussion.
I have never had a liking for they helmets anyway.*

*The old regiment did fine in the last attack. They
were specially mentioned in Orders next day. The
objective was reached under heavy fire and position
consolidated before we were relieved next morning.*

"Good boys!" interpolated Bobby softly.

*Colonel Carmichael, late of the Second Battn., I
think, is now in command. A very nice gentleman,
but we have all been missing you and the Captain.*

*They tell me that I will be for home service after
this. My head is doing well, but the muscules of my
right leg is badly torn. I should have liked fine for
to have stayed out and come home with the other boys
when we are through with Berlin.*

*Having no more to say, sir, I will now draw to a
close.*

                                    Jas. Mucklewame,
                                         C.S.M.

After the perusal of this characteristic *Ave
atque Vale!* the two friends adjourned to the bal-
cony, overlooking the Green Park. Here they lit
their cigars in reminiscent silence, while neigh-

bouring search-lights raked the horizon for Zeppelins which no longer came. It was a moment for confidences.

"Old Mucklewame is like the rest of us," said Wagstaffe at last.

"How?"

"Wanting to go back, and all that. I do too — just because I'm here, I suppose. A year ago, out there, my chief ambition was to get home, with a comfortable wound and a comfortable conscience."

"Same here," admitted Bobby.

"It was the same with practically every one," said Wagstaffe. "If any man asserts that he really enjoys modern warfare, after, say, six months of it, he is a liar. In the South African show I can honestly say I was perfectly happy. We were fighting in open country, against an adversary who was a gentleman; and although there was plenty of risk, the chances were that one came through all right. At any rate, there was no poison gas, and one did not see a whole platoon blown to pieces, or buried alive, by a single shell. If Brother Boer took you prisoner, he did not stick you in the stomach with a saw-edged bayonet. At the worst he pinched your trousers. But Brother Boche is a different proposition. Since he butted in, war has descended in the social scale. And modern scientific developments have turned a sporting chance of being scuppered into a mathematical certainty. And yet — and yet — old Mucklewame is right. One *hates* to be out of it — especially at the finish. When the regiment comes stumping through London on its way

back to Euston — next year, or whenever it's
going to be — with their ragged pipers leading
the way, you would like to be at the head of 'A'
Company, Bobby, and I would give something to
be exercising my old function of whipper-in. Eh,
boy?"

"Never mind," said practical Bobby. "Perhaps we shall be on somebody's glittering Staff.
What I hate to feel at present is that the other
fellows, out there, have got to go on sticking it,
while we —"

"And by God," exclaimed Wagstaffe, "what
stickers they are — and were! Did you ever see
anything so splendid, Bobby, as those six-months-
old soldiers of ours — in the early days, I mean,
when we held our trenches, week by week, under
continuous bombardment, and our gunners behind could only help us with four or five rounds a
day?"

"I never did," said Bobby, truthfully.

"I admit to you," continued Wagstaffe, "that
when I found myself pitchforked into 'K (1)'
at the outbreak of the war, instead of getting
back to my old line battalion, I was a pretty sick
man. I hated everybody. I was one of the old
school — or liked to think I was — and the ways
of the new school were not my ways. I hated the
new officers. Some of them bullied the men; some
of them allowed themselves to be bullied by
N.C.O.'s. Some never gave or returned salutes,
others went about saluting everybody. Some came
into Mess in fancy dress of their own design, and
elbowed senior officers off the hearthrug. I used

to marvel at the Colonel's patience with them.
But many of them are dead now, Bobby, and
they nearly all made good. Then the men! After
ten years in the regular Army I hated them all —
the way they lounged, the way they dressed, the
way they sat, the way they spat. I wondered
how I could ever go on living with them. And
now — I find myself wondering how I am ever
going to live without them. We shall not see their
like again. The new lot — present lot — are
splendid fellows. They are probably better soldiers. Certainly they are more uniformly trained.
But there was a piquancy about our old scamps in
'K (1)' that was unique — priceless — something
the world will never see again."

"I don't know," said Bobby thoughtfully.
"That Cockney regiment which lay beside us at
Albert last summer was a pretty priceless lot.
Do you remember a pair of fat fellows in their
leading platoon? We called them Fortnum and
Mason!"

"I do — particularly Fortnum. Go on!"

"Well, their bit of trench was being shelled one
day, and Fortnum, who was in number one bay
with five other men, kept shouting out to Mason,
who was round a traverse and out of sight, to en-
quire how he was getting on. 'Are you all right,
Bill?' 'Are you *sure* you're all right, Bill?'
'Are you *still* all right, Bill?' and so on. At last
Bill, getting fed up with this unusual solicitude,
yelled back: 'What's all the anxiety abaht, eh?'
And Fortnum put his head round the traverse and explained. 'We're getting up a little

sweepstake in our bay,' he said, 'abaht the first casuality, and I've drawn you, ole son!'"

Wagstaffe chuckled.

"That must have been the regiment that had the historic poker party," he said.

"What yarn was that?"

"I heard it from the Brigadier — four times, to be exact. Five men off duty were sitting in a dugout playing poker. A gentleman named 'Erb had just gone to the limit on his hand, when a riflegrenade came into the dug-out from somewhere and did him in. While they were waiting for the stretcher-bearers, one of the other players picked up 'Erb's hand and examined it. Then he laid it down again, and said: 'It does n't matter, chaps. Poor 'Erb would n't a made it, anyway. I 'ad four queens.'"

"Tommy has his own ideas of fun, I'll admit," said Bobby. "Do you remember those first trenches of ours at Festubert? There was a dead Frenchman buried in the parapet — you know how they used to bury people in those days?"

"I did notice it. Go on."

"Well, this poor chap's hand stuck out, just about four feet from the floor of the trench. My dug-out was only a few yards away, and I never saw a member of my platoon go past that spot without shaking the hand and saying, 'Goodmorning, Alphonse!' I had it built up with sandbags ultimately, and they were quite annoyed!"

"They have some grisly notions about life and death," agreed Wagstaffe, "but they are extraordi-

narily kind to people in trouble, such as wounded
men, or prisoners. You can't better them."

"And now there are five millions of them.
We are all in it, at last!"

"We certainly are — men and women. I'm
afraid I had hardly realised what our women were
doing for us. Being on service all the time, one
rather overlooks what is going on at home. But
stopping a bullet puts one in the way of a good
deal of inside information on that score."

"You mean hospital work, and so on?"

"Yes. One meets a lot of wonderful people that
way! Sisters, and ward-maids, and V.A.D.'s —"

"I love all V.A.D.'s!" said Bobby, unexpect-
edly.

"Why, my youthful Mormon?"

"Because they are the people who do all the
hard work and get no limelight — like — like —!"

"Like Second Lieutenants — eh?"

"Yes, that is the idea. They have a pretty
hard time, you know," continued Bobby confidentially: "And nothing heroic, either. Giving up all
the fun that a girl is entitled to; washing dishes;
answering the door-bell; running up and down-
stairs; eating rotten food. That's the sort of —"

"What is her name?" enquired the accusing
voice of Major Wagstaffe. Then, without waiting to extort an answer from the embarrassed
Bobby: —

"You are quite right. This war has certainly
brought out the best in our women. The South
African War brought out the worst. My good-
ness, you should have seen the Mount Nelson

Hotel at Capetown in those days! But they
have been wonderful this time — wonderful. I
love them all — the bus-conductors, the ticket-
punchers, the lift-girls — one of them nearly shot
me right through the roof of Harrod's the other
day — and the window-cleaners and the page-
girls and the railway-portresses! I divide my
elderly heart among them. And I met a bunch
of munition girls the other day, Bobby, coming
home from work. They were all young, and most
of them were pretty. Their faces and hands were
stained a bright orange-colour with picric acid,
and will be, I suppose, until the Boche is booted
back into his stye. In other words, they had de-
liberately sacrificed their good looks for the duration of the war. That takes a bit of doing, I
know, innocent bachelor though I am. But bless
you, they were n't worrying. They waved their
orange-coloured hands to me, and pointed to
their orange-coloured faces, and laughed. They
were *proud* of them; they were doing their bit.
They nearly made me cry, Bobby. Yes, we are
all in it now; and those of us who come out of it
are going to find this old island of ours a wonderfully changed place to live in."

"How? Why?" enquired Bobby. Possibly he
was interested in Wagstaffe's unusual expansive-
ness: possibly he hoped to steer the conversation away from the topic of V.A.D.'s — possibly
towards it. You never know.

"Well," said Wagstaffe, "we are all going to
understand one another a great deal better after
this war."

"Who? Labour and Capital, and so on?"

"'Labour and Capital' is a meaningless and misleading expression, Bobby. For instance, our men regard people like you and me as Capitalists; the ordinary Brigade Major regards us as Labourers, and pretty common Labourers at that. It is all a question of degree. But what I mean is this. You can't call your employer a tyrant and an extortioner after he has shared his rations with you and never spared himself over your welfare and comfort through weary months of trench-warfare; neither, when you have experienced a working-man's courage and cheerfulness and reliability in the day of battle, can you turn round and call him a loafer and an agitator in time of peace — can you? That is just what the *Bandar-log* overlook, when they jabber about the dreadful industrial upheaval that is coming with peace. Most of all have they overlooked the fact that with the coming of peace this country will be invaded by several million of the wisest men that she has ever produced — the New British Army. That Army will consist of men who have spent three years in getting rid of mutual misapprehensions and assimilating one another's point of view — men who went out to the war ignorant and intolerant and insular, and are coming back wise to all the things that really matter. They will flood this old country, and they will make short work of the agitator, and the alarmist, and the profiteer, and all the nasty creatures that merely make a noise instead of *doing* something, and who crab the work of the

Army and Navy — more especially the Navy — because there is n't a circus victory of some kind in the paper every morning. Yes, Bobby, when our boys get back, and begin to ask the *Bandar-log* what they *did* in the Great War — well, it's going to be a rotten season for *Bandar-log* generally!"

There was silence again. Presently Bobby spoke: —

"When our boys get back! Some of them are never coming back again, worse luck!"

"Still," said Wagstaffe, "what they did was worth doing, and what they died for was worth while. I think their one regret to-day would be that they did not live to see their own fellows taking the offensive — the line going forward on the Somme; the old tanks waddling over the Boche trenches; and the Boche prisoners throwing up their hands and yowling 'Kamerad'! And the Kut unpleasantness cleaned up, and all the kinks in the old Salient straightened out! And Wytchaete and Messines! You remember how the two ridges used to look down into our lines at Wipers and Plugstreet? And now we're on top of both of them! Some of our friends out there — the friends who are not coming back — would have liked to know about that, Bobby. I wish they could, somehow."

"Perhaps they do," said Bobby simply.

It was close on midnight. Our "two old soldiers, broken in the wars," levered themselves stiffly to their feet, and prepared to depart.

"Heigho!" said Wagstaffe. "It is time for two

old wrecks like us to be in bed. That's what we
are, Bobby — wrecks, dodderers, has-beens! But
we have had the luck to last longer than most.
We have dodged the missiles of the Boche to an
extent which justifies us in claiming that we have
followed the progress of their war with a rather
more than average degree of continuity. We were
the last of the old crowd, too. Kemp has got his
Brigade, young Cockerell has gone to be a Staff
Captain, and — you and I are here. Some of the
others dropped out far too soon. Young Lochgair,
old Blaikie —"

"Waddell, too," said Bobby. "We joined the
same day."

"And Angus M'Lachlan. I think he would
have made the finest soldier of the lot of us,"
added Wagstaffe. "You remember his remark to
me, that we only had the bye to play now? He
was a true prophet: we are dormy, anyhow. (Only
cold feet at Home can let us down now.) And he
only saw three months' service! Still, he made a
great exit from this world, Bobby, and that is
the only thing that matters in these days. Ha!
H'm! As our new Allies would say, I am beginning to 'pull heart stuff' on you. Let us go to
bed. Sleeping here?"

"Yes, till to-morrow. Then off on leave."

"How much have you got?"

"A month. I say?"

"Yes?"

"Are you doing anything on the nineteenth?"

Wagstaffe regarded his young friend suspi-
ciously.

"Is this a catch of some kind?" he enquired.

"Oh, no. Will you be my —" Bobby turned excessively pink, and completed his request.

Wagstaffe surveyed him resignedly.

"We all come to it, I suppose," he observed. "Only some come to it sooner than others. Are you of age, my lad? Have your parents —"

"I'm twenty-two," said Bobby shortly.

"Will the bridesmaids be pretty?"

"They are all peaches," replied Bobby, with enthusiasm. "But nothing whatever," he added, in a voice of respectful rapture, "compared with the bride!"

THE END

www.ingramcontent.com/pod-product-compliance
Lightning Source LLC
Chambersburg PA
CBHW050507260626
47157CB00004B/1228